Third Strike
by

Kathi Daley

Acknowledgments

I want to thank the very talented Jessica Fischer for the cover art.

I so appreciate Bruce Curran, who is always ready and willing to answer my cyber questions, Jayme Maness who takes charge of book clubs and other reader events, and Peggy Hyndman for helping sleuth out those pesky typos.

And, of course, thanks to the readers and bloggers in my life, who make doing what I do possible.

Thank you to Randy Ladenheim-Gil for the editing.

And finally I want to thank my sister Christy for always lending an ear and my husband Ken for allowing me time to write by taking care of everything else.

Books by Kathi Daley

Come for the murder, stay for the romance.

Zoe Donovan Cozy Mystery:

Halloween Hijinks
The Trouble With Turkeys
Christmas Crazy
Cupid's Curse
Big Bunny Bump-off
Beach Blanket Barbie
Maui Madness
Derby Divas
Haunted Hamlet
Turkeys, Tuxes, and Tabbies
Christmas Cozy
Alaskan Alliance
Matrimony Meltdown
Soul Surrender
Heavenly Honeymoon
Hopscotch Homicide
Ghostly Graveyard
Santa Sleuth
Shamrock Shenanigans
Kitten Kaboodle
Costume Catastrophe
Candy Cane Caper
Holiday Hangover
Easter Escapade
Camp Carter
Trick or Treason – *September 2017*
Reindeer Roundup – *December 2017*

Zimmerman Academy The New Normal
Ashton Falls Cozy Cookbook

Tj Jensen Paradise Lake Mysteries by Henery Press

Pumpkins in Paradise
Snowmen in Paradise
Bikinis in Paradise
Christmas in Paradise
Puppies in Paradise
Halloween in Paradise
Treasure in Paradise
Fireworks in Paradise – *October 2017*

Whales and Tails Cozy Mystery:

Romeow and Juliet
The Mad Catter
Grimm's Furry Tail
Much Ado About Felines
Legend of Tabby Hollow
Cat of Christmas Past
A Tale of Two Tabbies
The Great Catsby
Count Catula
The Cat of Christmas Present
A Winter's Tail
The Taming of the Tabby
Frankencat – *August 2017*
The Cat of Christmas Future – *November 2017*

Seacliff High Mystery:
The Secret
The Curse
The Relic
The Conspiracy
The Grudge
The Shadow
The Haunting – *September 2017*

Sand and Sea Hawaiian Mystery:
Murder at Dolphin Bay
Murder at Sunrise Beach
Murder at the Witching Hour
Murder at Christmas
Murder at Turtle Cove
Murder at Water's Edge
Murder at Midnight – *October 2017*

Writers' Retreat Southern Seashore Mystery:
First Case
Second Look
Third Strike
Fourth Victim – *October 2017*

Rescue Alaska Paranormal Mystery
Finding Justice – *November 2017*

Road to Christmas Romance:
Road to Christmas Past

The Writers:

Jillian (Jill) Hanford

Jillian is a dark-haired, dark-eyed, never-married newspaper reporter who moved to Gull Island after her much-older brother, Garrett Hanford, had a stroke and was no longer able to run the resort he'd inherited. Jillian had suffered a personal setback and needed a change in lifestyle, so she decided to run the resort as a writers' retreat while she waited for an opportunity to work her way back into her old life. To help make ends meet, she takes on freelance work that allows her to maintain her ties to the newspaper industry. Jillian shares her life with her partner in mystery solving, an ornery parrot with an uncanny ability to communicate named Blackbeard.

Jackson (Jack) Jones

Jack is a dark-haired, blue-eyed, never-married nationally acclaimed author of hard-core mysteries and thrillers, who is as famous for his good looks and boyish charm as he is for the stories he pens. Despite his success as a novelist, he'd always dreamed of writing for a newspaper, so he gave up his penthouse apartment and bought the failing *Gull Island News*. He lives in an oceanfront mansion he pays for with income from the novels he continues to write.

George Baxter

George is a writer of traditional whodunit mysteries. He'd been a friend of Garrett Hanford's since they were boys and spent many winters at the resort penning his novels. When he heard that the oceanfront resort was going to be used as a writers' retreat, he was one of the first to get on board. George is a distinguished-looking man with gray hair, dark green eyes, and a certain sense of old-fashioned style that many admire.

Clara Kline

Clara is a self-proclaimed psychic who writes fantasy and paranormal mysteries. She wears her long gray hair in a practical braid and favors long, peasant-type skirts and blouses. Clara decided to move to the retreat after she had a vision that she would find her soul mate living within its walls. So far, the only soul mate she has stumbled on to is a cat named Agatha, but it does seem that romance is in the air, so she may yet find the man she has envisioned.

Alex Cole

Alex is a fun and flirty millennial who made his first million writing science fiction when he was just twenty-two. He's the lighthearted jokester of the group who uses his blond-haired, blue-eyed good looks to participate in serial dating. He has the means to live anywhere, but the thought of a writers' retreat seemed quaint and retro, so he decided to expand his base of experience and moved in.

Brit Baxter

Brit is George Baxter's niece. A petite blond pixie, she decided to make the trip east with her uncle after quitting her job to pursue her dream of writing. She's a MIT graduate who decided her real love was writing.

Victoria Vance

Victoria is a romance author who lives the life she writes about in her steamy novels. She travels the world and does what she wants to who she wants without ever making an emotional connection. Her raven-black hair accentuates her pale skin and bright green eyes. When she isn't traveling the world she's Jillian's best friend, which is why when Jillian needed her, she gave up her penthouse apartment overlooking Central Park to move into the dilapidated island retreat.

Townsfolk:

Deputy Rick Savage

Rick is not only the island's main source of law enforcement, he's a volunteer force unto himself. He cares about the island and its inhabitants and is willing to do what needs to be done to protect that which he loves. He's single man in his thirties who seldom has time to date despite his devilish good looks, which most believe could land him any woman he wants.

Mayor Betty Sue Bell

Betty Sue is a homegrown Southern lady who owns a beauty parlor called Betty Boop's Beauty Salon. She can be flirty and sassy, but when her town or its citizens are in trouble, she turns into a barracuda. She has a southern flare that will leave you laughing, but when there's a battle to fight she's the one you most want in your corner.

Gertie Newsome

Gertie Newsome is the owner of Gertie's on the Wharf. Southern born and bred, she believes in the magic of the South and the passion of its people. She shares her home with a ghost named Mortie who has been a regular part of her life for over thirty years. She's friendly, gregarious, and outspoken, unafraid to take on anyone or anything she needs to protect those she loves.

Meg Collins

Meg is a volunteer at the island museum and the organizer of the turtle rescue squad. Some feel the island and its wildlife are her life, but Meg has a soft spot for island residents like Jill and the writers who live with her.

Barbara Jean Freeman

Barbara is an outspoken woman with a tendency toward big hair and loud colors. She is a friendly sort with a propensity toward gossip who owns a bike shop in town.

Sully

Sully is a popular islander who owns the local bar.

The Victim

Trey Alderman

Trey Alderman was probably Gull Island's most important claim to sports fame. He was the starting pitcher for the Gull Island Seagulls and went on to stand out nationally among college players while attending the University of South Carolina. It was assumed he would be a top draft pick and it seemed the sky was the limit in terms of his career until he died of a heart attack when he was only twenty-two. It was later determined there was a drug mixture in his system that could lead to a heart attack when combined with extreme stress.

The Suspects and Witnesses

Friends from Gull Island who attended the party:

Heather Granger

Trey's girlfriend all through high school. Everyone assumed they would marry one day, but when he left his small town behind in his search for national recognition, he left Heather behind as well. She is now engaged to a chef and opening her own restaurant.

Hudson Dickerson

Trey's best friend in high school, who stayed behind to work on his father's fishing boat when Trey went off to college. The two were still close. Hudson married his longtime girlfriend, Candy, and still lives on Gull Island.

Candy Baldwin

Heather's best friend and Hudson's girlfriend. Many felt Candy was angrier at Trey for dumping Heather than even she was. The two couples had been inseparable at one time and Candy had dreamed of a shared future.

Dexter Parkway

Trey's nerdy friend who attended Boston College but, like Trey, was home on spring break. In high school Dexter had idolized Trey, although Trey treated him more like a faithful dog than a friend. He's currently working on his doctorate at Harvard.

Coach Cranston

Trey's high school coach, who helped him hone his skills. Trey had promised him that if he made it big, he would hire him as his agent, but as his fame grew, so did his ambition. It was rumored Trey had left Coach Cranston in the dust in favor of a flashy agent with proven experience.

Friends from college who attended the party:

Rena Madison

Trey's college girl and a cheerleader at the University of South Carolina. Rena had big plans that would be more easily accomplished with a professional baseball player on her arm. Unlike Heather, who seemed to love Trey for who he was, Rena was in it for what he could do for her modeling career. Rumor had it that Trey planned to dump her as soon as he graduated from college.

Jett Strong

Trey's biggest rival for the top spot in college baseball. Trey and Jett had traded the number one and two spots the entire four years they played. Most assumed one or the other would be the number one draft pick and college MVP. After Trey's death, Jett moved into the number one spot and currently plays for the Florida Marlins.

Parker Wilson

Trey's teammate, who would have had an outstanding college career of his own had he managed to get out from under Trey's shadow. After Trey's death, he married his college girlfriend, Quinn, and was drafted to the New York Yankees.

Quinn Jenkins

Quinn Jenkins also attended the University of South Carolina and was Parker's girlfriend. An assertive woman majoring in microbiology, she felt Parker was getting a raw deal and had been campaigning hard with the coach to offer him more playing time and a starting position. She knew Parker had what it took to live in the spotlight if only Trey wasn't in the way.

Chapter 1

Wednesday, November 15

Trey Alderman was Gull Island's most important claim to sports fame. He was the starting pitcher for the Gull Island Seagulls and went on to stand out nationally among college players while attending the University of South Carolina. It was assumed he would be a top draft pick a year and a half back, and it seemed the sky was the limit in terms of his career. Trey came home on spring break during his senior year and, while on the island, agreed to play in a charity event in Charleston. The game, which featured other draft hopefuls, came down to a single run. It was the bottom of the ninth, the tying run was on third, the bases were loaded, there were two outs, and the tension was high. The pitch was thrown fast and down the middle and the crowd held their breath as Trey swung his bat with all his might before falling to the ground. He was pronounced dead at the scene. It was later determined he died of a heart attack. He was twenty-two, healthy, and, as far as anyone knew, had no preexisting heart condition.

It was later revealed that Trey had arrived at the game feeling dizzy and disoriented. He'd elected to suit up but wasn't in the starting lineup. He'd begun to feel better as the game progressed, and by the ninth inning he was feeling amped and ready to play, so the coach put him in as a pinch hitter in the bottom of the ninth. The autopsy revealed that Trey didn't have an undiagnosed heart condition, as everyone had believed, but had been suffering the ill effects of a drug mixture in his system that could have led to a heart attack when combined with extreme stress. The local investigators determined that he had most likely engaged in recreational drug use at a party he'd attended the previous evening.

Alex Cole, a twenty-eight-year-old, fun and flirty millennial who'd made his first million writing science fiction when he was just twenty-two, had decided to write a book about Trey's life and death and had brought the mystery of Trey's death to the Mystery Mastermind group made up of people who lived and worked at the Gull Island Writers' Retreat, which my brother, Garrett Hanford, owns, and I, Jillian Hanford, operate.

"On the surface, it seems as if Trey's death was the result of his own poor choices," I pointed out. "I guess my question is: Where's the mystery?"

"There are those, including Trey's parents, who believe he didn't knowingly consume the drugs that led to his death," Alex answered.

"They think someone slipped him the drugs without his knowledge?" I clarified.

"Exactly. It's my intention to dig into the twenty-four hours leading up to his collapse and try to determine if Trey's death really was nothing more than a terrible accident or if he was murdered."

"You're suggesting whoever slipped Trey the drugs, if that's even what happened, knew they would cause his heart to fail?" I asked.

"Not necessarily. Trey's heart attack seems to have been the result of a very specific set of circumstances that couldn't have been planned or predicted, so my use of the word *murdered* is probably a bit more melodramatic than the situation warrants. Still, I do believe someone could have slipped Trey the drugs with the intention of making him ill enough that he'd miss the game."

"Have you had a chance to narrow down the lists of suspects and witnesses we need to follow up with?" Brit Baxter, a twenty-six-year-old chick lit writer and the newest member of our group asked.

"I have nine names I think should give us a starting point," Alex said as his long blond hair fell over his bright blue eyes. "Everyone on the list attended the same party Trey did the night before he died, all attended the game, and all had at least somewhat of a motive for wanting Trey out of the way."

I grabbed a bright red marker and stood in front of whiteboard, prepared to take notes as the discussion unfolded. We'd found that writing everything down permitted us to look at situations from a variety of perspectives and, in the end, helped us make sense of what usually began as a lot of unrelated information.

"I'll start with the residents of Gull Island who attended the party," Alex began as the group listened intently. "Fortunately, four of these five people still live on the island and are willing to speak to us when we're ready to begin our investigation."

"You've already spoken to everyone on the list?" asked George Baxter, a sixty-eight-year-old writer of traditional whodunits.

"I've spoken very briefly to more than half the people on the list so far," Alex confirmed. "I figured it would save us some time if I did a bit of the legwork ahead of time."

"Okay," I said, marker in hand. "Who do you have?"

"Heather Granger dated Trey Alderman all though high school. It was assumed Trey and she would marry at some point, and Heather had even applied to the University of South Carolina and sent in her acceptance there as soon as she found out that was the school he'd decided on. Shortly after their high school graduation, Trey broke up with her. He offered the standard we're-entering-a-new-phase-in-our-lives speech and asked her if she wanted to consider attending one of the other schools where she'd been accepted to make things less awkward."

"What a creep," Brit said with a hint of disgust in her voice. "If he didn't want his old girlfriend to interfere with his groove, *he* should have changed schools."

"The University of South Carolina was Trey's choice in the first place," Alex pointed out. "Heather was only going there to follow him."

"Whatever." Brit rolled her eyes.

"So what did Heather decide to do?" I asked to prevent an all-out argument. "Did she change schools?"

"She didn't go to college at all. From what I understand, she was pretty broken up when Trey dumped her from out of the blue, and most of the people I've spoken to said she sank into a bit of a depression. She has, however, gotten on with her life since then," Alex assured us, looking directly at Brit. "She's engaged to a chef she met just after Trey's death and they've bought that old storefront on the wharf and are opening a restaurant."

"If she has moved on, why is she on your list?" Brit asked.

"Because she hadn't moved on at the time of the party. In fact, I've heard she was quite enraged when Trey showed up with his new girlfriend, Rena Madison."

"Tell us about Rena," Brit suggested.

Alex hesitated. "I'd planned to cover the locals first and then move on to the visitors to the island who attended the party."

"It's okay. I can hop back and forth between the two lists, and I'd like to hear about Rena as well," I said encouragingly.

"Okay," Alex agreed, sorting through his notes. "Rena Madison was a popular cheerleader at the University of South Carolina. She started dating Trey when they were both juniors. From what I could find out, she's both beautiful and popular, and while she was majoring in communication, she had big plans to make a name for herself in modeling. While she didn't say as much to me, based on what others have told me, Rena was using Trey to advance her career. I can't speak to what was actually in her heart, but Trey's best friend from high school, Hudson Dickerson, shared with me that Trey planned to dump

Rena as soon as he was drafted, so in a way it appears they were using each other."

"Like I said, the guy was an ass." Brit's eyes flashed with annoyance. "Why are we trying to find out what happened to him again?"

"You're helping me write a book based on a set of circumstances I'm exploring. Trey Alderman may not be a sympathetic character, but I do find him an interesting one."

"Oh, right. Okay, continue."

I could see Trey's cavalier attitude toward the women he dated had become a sore spot for Brit. It would appear the blond-haired pixie was a lot more of a romantic than she let on.

"Do we have reason to believe Rena knew Trey planned to dump her?" asked Jackson Jones, a never-married, forty-two-year-old, nationally acclaimed author of hard-core mysteries and thrillers, who was as famous for his good looks and boyish charm as he was for the stories he penned. Jackson currently lived on Gull Island as mild-mannered Jack Jones, small-town newspaper owner.

"I spoke to a woman named Candy Baldwin. She was and still is Heather's best friend and has lived on the island all her life. She said Rena *did* know what Trey planned and had told everyone at the party she'd find a way to get her revenge."

"Do you have the sense Candy is someone whose word can be trusted?" Jack asked.

Alex shrugged "I'm not sure. She's a nice enough woman who's since married her own high school boyfriend, Hudson Dickerson."

"Trey's best friend?" I clarified.

"Yes. It seems all through high school Trey and Heather and Hudson and Candy weren't only best friends but best couple friends. It's been suggested to me that Candy took Trey's breakup with Heather and the end of their little group almost harder than Heather did. I can't say for certain yet, but it seems Candy might hold a pretty big grudge against the victim, so I guess I'd take anything she tells you with a grain of salt."

"Should Candy and Hudson both be added to the suspect list?" I wondered.

Alex nodded his head. "I would definitely consider Candy a suspect at this point. Hudson was Trey's best friend; as far as I can tell, he didn't have a motive to want to hurt him, but he was at the party and the game, so at the very least he's a witness. Add him to the list of people we should follow up with."

I made a few notes on the whiteboard, then asked Alex to go on.

"There are two locals we haven't discussed yet," he said. "Dexter Parkway was a bit of a nerd in high school, went on to pursue a career in computer science, and is currently working on a doctorate at Harvard. While in high school, he was an unpopular geek who saw Trey as something of a hero. Dexter idolized Trey and spent quite a lot of time not only following him around but doing his homework, while Trey treated him like a trained dog."

Brit didn't say a word, but I saw her face was quickly becoming an interesting shade of scarlet.

"If Dexter idolized Trey, why would he kill him?" asked Victoria Vance, a thirty-seven-year-old romance author and my best friend.

"I'm not saying he killed Trey, but keep in mind Dexter was in his final year of undergraduate work at Boston College at the time Trey died. The guy's really smart. I bet by the time he was twenty-two he must have realized his own worth and grown out of his need to idolize an athletic bully. Again, I only spoke to each of the people on my list for a brief time to get a general background, but it seems to me that by the time that party rolled around, Dexter should have been well past the point of being happy being someone's lapdog."

"So you think he could have drugged Trey to get back at him for the way he treated him in high school?" Victoria asked.

"I'm not ready to say that, but Dexter would have had a legitimate complaint, and he's one of the few people on the list who could have had the knowledge to put together the drug cocktail the police believe ended up killing Trey."

Everyone paused to let that sink in. While it was true you could get almost any information on the Web these days, it sounded like the drugs that killed Trey were pretty specific. I wondered if anyone else on the list had a background in chemistry or medicine, so I asked the question.

"Actually, yes. There's another person on the list with the expertise to concoct such a drug cocktail. Her name is Quinn Jenkins, but let me circle back around to her. First, I want to mention Coach Cranston."

"The baseball coach over at the high school?" Jack asked.

"Yes. Coach Cranston has been the coach for a number of years and was Trey's coach when he was in high school," Alex said.

"Trey was a star. Cranston must have loved him."

Alex nodded to Jack. "He did then. In fact, he put in a lot of extra time helping Trey hone his skills. He even managed to get him recognition from other coaches he knew in other parts of the country. The issue was, Trey more or less promised Coach Cranston that if he helped him get a college scholarship, he would take Cranston with him when he went pro. He promised to make him his agent. But when the time came to look for an adviser, he decided he needed someone flashier, someone with more experience. It was while he was home on spring break that he told Cranston he'd decided to go a different way."

"I bet he was angry," Clara Kline, a sixty-two-year-old self-proclaimed psychic and the writer of fantasy and paranormal mysteries, commented.

"From what I've heard, he was. Very angry. He'd stayed in contact with Trey all through his college career, treated him like a son, and discussed their plans for the future on many occasions. Trey's announcement that he was going with someone he'd just met seemed to come from out of left field. I understand Coach Cranston was not only angry but hurt as well."

"Have you considered a scenario where they *all* conspired to drug him?" I asked as the grudges against Trey piled up fast.

"Hang on; I haven't even gotten to the best suspects yet."

"Okay, spill," Brit encouraged. "Who do you think had the strongest reason to kill Trey Alderman?"

"Two other baseball players come to mind. Both were at the party, both played in the charity game during which Trey died, and both improved in ranking with Trey's death. Jett Strong attended Florida State University and was nationally ranked number two behind Trey. The rivalry between Jett and Trey was fierce, and each felt they deserved the title of MVP. During their four years of college, the two traded the number one spot a few times, but as of the day Trey died, it looked like he was going to edge out his rival and come out on top."

"And did Jett finish number one once Trey was out of the picture?" I asked.

"He did."

I jotted down a few notes. "You said there were two rivals?"

"Parker Wilson was the other one. He attended the University of South Carolina with Trey and was his teammate. He was a very good player in his own right, but he couldn't quite compete with Trey, who always stole the spotlight. Many people felt if Parker had been on a different team he would have been a star, but as Trey's teammate, he never got the attention he deserved."

"I bet that sucked," Brit said.

"I'm sure it did," Alex agreed.

"Why didn't Parker just transfer to another school?" I asked.

"It isn't that easy to transfer once you're committed to a sports program, plus he was attending the university on a scholarship," Alex explained.

"Now, what about this Quinn you were going to circle back to?" Brit asked.

Alex shuffled through his notes. "Quinn Jenkins also attended the University of South Carolina and was Parker's girlfriend. An assertive woman majoring in microbiology who felt Parker was getting a raw deal, she wasn't afraid to let anyone who would listen know about it. There are people I've interviewed who felt Quinn was exactly the kind of person to remove obstacles in her way, no matter what it took. For the rest of the season following Trey's death, Parker became the star of the team and was drafted by the New York Yankees. I understand he's building a pretty spectacular career with Quinn at his side."

I completed my notes, then took a step back from the whiteboard. We really had a daunting task ahead of us.

"Do you have a plan?" George asked.

"I know you're all busy with your own lives and careers, so I thought maybe you could tackle the suspects who live on the island, while I go after the ones who live out of state. Parker and Quinn live in New York, which is where I plan to start."

"And Jett?" I asked. "Was he drafted?"

"Yes; to the Florida Marlins. The season is over, so I'm not sure whether he'll be in Florida, but I'll track him down."

"And Rena?" I asked.

"She moved to New York to pursue her modeling career. I'll catch her at the same time I visit Parker and Quinn. I'm planning to leave for New York tomorrow. I'd love to get the interviews and other research wrapped up before Thanksgiving if possible."

"Okay; I'm game to jump right in," I said to the group.

"Me too," Jack seconded.

"I'll consult my cards," Clara promised. "I think this is going to be a juicy one. I can already sense lies and deceit. If I had to guess, the true motive behind Trey's death is still buried deep beneath the surface of the cruelty and betrayal he left behind. Agatha," Clara said, referring to her cat, "thinks there may be another player not yet identified."

"Please have Agatha let us know as soon as she figures out who we're missing," Alex said gently.

"Oh, I will, dear. This is quite a task you're taking on and we're happy to help. Aren't we, Agatha?"

"Meow," answered the cat, sitting primly in Clara's lap.

"And I'll dig in with my research," George promised. "I have several ideas already."

"I'll build a social media map," Brit offered. "I've found them to come in handy."

"I don't know how I can help, but I'm in as well," Victoria offered.

"Great," I said after everyone had chimed in. I looked at Blackbeard, my very opinionated and very intuitive parrot, who seemed to be able to communicate his thoughts and feelings. "How about it, big guy? You up for another mystery?"

Blackbeard didn't respond, which was uncharacteristic of him.

I turned back to the others, "I guess he doesn't have anything to say. Can everyone meet back here on Monday evening? That will give us time to do some digging around."

Everyone agreed Monday would be fine. Jack was going to make some calls the next day, and then he and I would get started with interviews on Friday. Hopefully, once we began speaking to people, a pattern would emerge.

"Before everyone goes, I wanted to give you an update on the cabin situation," I said. "The inspector is coming tomorrow and I expect we'll receive the permits for the second three cabins." I looked directly at Victoria. "I know you plan to move into the largest of the three, but that still leaves two cabins I need to find tenants for." I turned toward Clara. "Are you sure you'd prefer to stay in the main house?"

"Yes, dear. Agatha and I are quite happy in our room on the second floor."

"Okay, then, I'll look for tenants for the other two cabins. I have a woman coming by tomorrow for an interview. Her name is Nicole Carrington and she's a true crime writer. I'm not certain she's interested in a long-term rental; so far, she's expressed interest in leasing a cabin for a few months while she does research in this area. I feel as if we're a family, so I wanted to be sure no one has had any negative experiences with her. I understand she can be assertive."

"Never heard of her," Brit said.

"I've never met her, but I've read her work," George offered. "She seems to be committed to telling the victim's story in much the way we do here. I found her research and conclusions to be thorough and well thought out. I have a feeling she'll fit in just fine."

I looked around at the others. "Anyone else have an opinion?"

No one spoke up, so I decided to go ahead with the interview to get a firsthand impression.

"Okay, then; I guess that's all I have." I glanced at Victoria. "You should be able to begin moving in tomorrow afternoon."

"Great. Who wants to help me move my stuff over?"

Everyone except Alex, who would be gone by then, agreed to help. Shortly after the group began to break up, I walked Jack to the door, then came back in to clean up.

"So what do you think?" Alex asked as I put away the dry erase markers I'd been using for the whiteboard.

"I think the mystery is intriguing and I believe the others are hooked as well, but I do wonder why you decided to write this specific book. You usually write science fiction. A biography seems out of your wheelhouse."

Alex shrugged. "I'm not sure what prompted me to write this book. I'm interested in sports, and Trey's story was one that captured national attention at the time of his death. The whole thing seemed odd to me, so I did some digging and realized I wanted to follow the clues wherever they might lead."

"Well, I'm glad you brought the mystery to the group. I've found working as a team to be quite satisfying."

"I'm glad you're in. I'm going to head out early in the morning, so I guess I'll see you on Sunday, Monday afternoon at the latest."

"Call me in a day or two to touch base."

"I will. I'm hoping we'll have the suspect list narrowed down a bit by this time next week."

I hoped Alex was right, though I'd found that when it came to researching cold cases, things were never as simple as they might initially seem.

Once everyone had gone off to their own cabin or room, I wrapped myself in a heavy sweater and headed out onto the deck. It was a clear night and the stars shone brightly in the dark sky. I sat down on one of the patio chairs and closed my eyes. I loved listening to the sound of the waves rolling onto the shore. I felt the tension melt from my body as the gentle rhythm eased the stress created by a phone call from my mother earlier in the day. I'd hoped she would agree to come to the island for Thanksgiving. She had yet to see my new home or meet my new friends. I also really wanted her to meet Garrett, the brother with whom I shared a father, even though I knew it was going to be a sensitive subject to address.

Of course, even though Mom admitted she wasn't busy over Thanksgiving, she made it clear she was much *too* busy to come to my little island. She invited me to fly out to join her in Los Angeles, but spending Thanksgiving with her Hollywood crowd sounded like the worst idea I'd heard in quite some time. There was no doubt about it; I'd just need to have my own dinner. Not that I had a clue where to start in preparing such a meal. Gertie Newsome, owner of Gertie's on the Wharf, had attended my Halloween dinner party; maybe she'd agree not only to spend Thanksgiving at the Turtle Cove Writers' Retreat but help with the planning and cooking as well.

"Beautiful night," I heard George say.

I opened my eyes. "It is. Are you out for a walk?"

"A short one. Walking helps to clear my mind so I can settle in without a million thoughts running through my head, disturbing my sleep. Mind if I sit with you for a minute?"

"Not at all. I'd welcome the company."

George sat down next to me. He took the old pipe he often smoked out of his pocket and held it up in question. I nodded, so he lit it and took a few puffs of the sweet-smelling tobacco. I wasn't a fan of cigarette or even cigar smoke, but I found the smoke from a pipe brought back fond memories of my grandfather.

George and I sat in silence for a few minutes before he spoke. "I was down at the museum today, talking to Meg Collins about the history of the island for the historical novel I'm writing."

He paused, and it seemed to me his thought was incomplete. "How did that go?" I asked.

"Good. Meg is a very bright woman. She had a lot of very useful information and she seemed very enthusiastic about sharing her love of the island. She really is quite remarkable."

"She is," I agreed.

"I was wondering if you knew much about her personal life."

I turned and looked directly at George. "Her personal life?"

"Marital status. That sort of thing."

I smiled. It looked as if George might have a crush on the turtle rescue lady. "I know she's currently single and that she has a daughter who lives out of state, so I imagine she must have been married at some point, although it's possible to have a child without a husband. She's lived on the island for a long time; I've had conversations with her in which she's shared memories of events that occurred here decades ago. I also know she's kind and intelligent and really cares about the island, the people who live here, and the turtles she protects."

"So you're certain she isn't currently involved in a romantic relationship?"

I placed my hand on George's arm. "No, I'm not certain. The subject's never come up between us, but based on what I've observed, I'd say she's very much single. If you want to know for certain, why don't you ask her?"

It was odd to see George, who was always so confident and levelheaded, stuttering around like a schoolboy.

"I've had a good life though I've never married and really haven't dated all that much. The pursuit of knowledge has always been my mistress, so asking out a woman I've only recently gotten to know feels awkward. Maybe I should just spend more time at the museum. Get to know her better."

"That's probably a good idea. I'm thinking of having a big Thanksgiving dinner here at the resort. I haven't asked everyone yet, but I'm fairly certain everyone plans to be around. Why don't you invite her? I don't know whether she already has plans, but if she doesn't, it'll give you the opportunity to get that first date out of the way while surrounded by people who know and love you."

George furrowed his brow. I could see he needed to give the idea some thought. "It would be a nice thing to invite her to have Thanksgiving with all of us if she doesn't have plans. I've spent a good number of holidays alone, and I can say from experience that being by yourself while others are with family and friends is a lonely proposition."

"I agree. Meg knows everyone at the retreat to a certain degree and I'm sure she'd be happy to have a place to go if she isn't already busy."

"Okay." I could see George had made up his mind. "I'll ask her tomorrow."

"Great. I'm going to invite all the writers here, along with Jack and Gertie, who I'm hoping will help with the cooking. Oh, and Deputy Savage, although he has family on the island, so he may be busy."

George chuckled. "Oh, I don't know about that. Judging by the way he and Victoria eye each other when they think no one's looking, I'd say there's a good chance he'll come if she'll be here."

George had a point. Rick Savage and Victoria had been tiptoeing around each other ever since she'd been back from Los Angeles, and I suspected it was only a matter of time before the cat-and-mouse dance they'd been engaged in turned into another sort of dance entirely.

Chapter 2

Thursday, November 16

Stan Barber was the most laid-back building inspector I'd ever met. When he'd come to inspect the three cabins George, Alex, and Brit had moved into a month ago, all he'd done was peek in the door of each unit before commenting on such trivial things as wall color and flooring choices. I'd been stressing over the first inspection for days, going over every little detail to make sure I had all my ducks in a row, but this time I prepared for Stan's visit by baking pumpkin muffins to offer the easygoing man.

"Mornin', Ms. Hanford," Stan greeted me as he climbed out of his beat-up old truck. "This here is my friend Gordo. I think I mentioned the last time that I might bring him by."

"Yes, I remember. I'm pleased to meet you, Gordo."

"This is a real nice place you have here." Gordo turned in a full circle after climbing out of the truck.

"Thank you. My brother owns it, but I'm very much enjoying living here." I turned to Stan. "The three cabins ready for inspection are just down this path. I've opened them up for you so you can look around at your leisure."

"Did you take my advice about the flooring?" Stan asked. He hadn't been a fan of the carpet we'd installed in the first three cabins.

"I did," I answered. "We've installed tile throughout. And, as with the first three cabins, the outside decks have been upgraded to commercial quality and all the appliances were installed by a professional."

"Okay, let's have a look."

I led Stan and Gordo down the narrow path that wound its way through the trees to the clearing where the second set of cabins were located. Initially, twenty cabins had been scattered around the large property Garrett owned, but after speaking to several contractors, we'd decided that eight of the twenty cabins would be torn down, leaving the twelve best to undergo renovations. We'd managed to complete six of the twelve in just four months and were set to begin another three as early as next week.

"I like the way the cabins are tucked into the trees so each space seems very private," Gordo commented.

"Yes, whoever originally designed the space did a good job. We tore down the cabins in the worst repair, which opened up the space even more than it was already."

"So you aren't planning to reopen the resort as a family vacation spot?"

"Not now," I answered Stan's friend. "We currently have six authors in residence and I have applications from several others who are interested in long- or short-term lodging."

"If I was an author, I'd be interested. Place is real nice and peaceful."

Stan paused as we arrived at the first of the three cabins. This time he actually went inside and did a cursory inspection. He checked all the electrical outlets and turned the water in the kitchen sink on and off. He opened the kitchen cupboards and asked a few questions about the circuit breakers and the emergency turnoff for the gas and water. Gordo decided to take a walk down to the beach while Stan worked, so I followed quietly behind him, answering any questions he had.

As it had been last time, this inspection was relatively painless. He offered a few suggestions as he worked, but I could see he hadn't found any problems. Once he'd completed his task, we headed back to his truck, where he signed the paperwork I'd need and I handed him a bag full of homemade muffins. Gordo returned from the beach just as we were finishing our conversation. He asked about the man working in the cabin closest to the beach, where the turtles laid their eggs, and I explained that the contractor was here today to prepare the next three cabins for the crew that would start work the following week. I assured both men that the renovations would be completed long before the turtles returned to the area next spring.

After they left, I headed down to the cabins that were being prepped to check in with the general contractor Garrett had hired.

"How does it look?" I asked as I entered the cabin in which he was working.

Jason Silverman was a tall man with broad shoulders who never smiled and seemed to totally lack a sense of humor. When I'd first met him, I'd found his tendency to take everything extremely seriously to be off-putting, but as I got to know him better I'd realized his structured approach to things was simply his way of processing the world around him. Under his gruff exterior, he was a pretty nice guy.

"Everything looks fine. I found this in the wall when I pulled the paneling away." Jason handed me a small metal box.

"This was in the wall?"

"Yes, ma'am. Looks like it's been there a while."

I tried to open it, but it was locked. "I suppose some past occupant must have left it there. I wonder why they didn't take it when they left."

"Don't rightly know. I looked around for a key but didn't find one."

I looked at the box I held in my hands. "I guess I can try to pick the lock. Maybe the name of the owner will be inside. Did you find anything else in the wall when you removed the paneling?"

"No, ma'am, just the box. I'm about through here for today. I have a crew scheduled to arrive on Monday to finish the demolition. They should be here for a day or two. The crew who'll take care of the new construction will start the Monday after Thanksgiving."

"That's great. I appreciate how fast you've gotten this project started."

"A fast turnaround was part of the contract I worked out with Garrett." Jason began stacking the old paneling outside the cabin for pickup later. "Did the inspection go all right?"

"Everything was fine. I have a writer moving in to the larger of the cabins this afternoon."

"Okay, then. I'll see you on Monday."

"Have a nice weekend." I waved as he headed to his truck. He waved back but didn't say anything. Not that I was expecting him to. Jason wasn't the sort to waste words on pleasantries.

I went to the main house and informed Vikki that she could begin moving her stuff in at any time. Then I took the box Jason had found up to my room. I had to admit I was curious about what might be inside. The box wasn't overly heavy, but I could hear things moving around inside, so I knew it wasn't empty. First, I tried to pick the lock with a nail file, but that didn't work, so I decided to see if I could find something to cut off the lock. I hated to ruin the box, but it was old and I was fairly certain whoever had left it hidden must have forgotten all about it.

"Do you know if we have bolt cutters anywhere?" I asked Clara, who was sitting on the sunporch drinking tea.

"I'm not sure. Maybe you should ask George. I know he has some tools he keeps on hand to make minor repairs."

"Is he in his cabin?"

"I believe so. How did the inspection go?"

"We're all set," I answered. "Vikki is packing her stuff as we speak."

I was about to head out to look for George when I realized Nicole Carrington was due to arrive at any moment. I informed Clara that our potential tenant would be here shortly and asked if she'd like to take part in the interview. Clara had moments when she demonstrated odd behavior that would put some people off, but she was also sensitive and observant and I welcomed her input. The current group of authors at the retreat had become very important to me and the last thing I wanted to do was make an addition that would upset the family we'd created.

******

Nicole Carrington was a tall woman with a thin frame and long black hair. She had a pale complexion and huge brown eyes that made her look startled much of the time. Like Jason, she had a serious and confident way about her that I suspected presented a barrier to others. I introduced Clara and myself, then asked Nicole to take a seat in the living room so we could chat.

"Before I show you the cabin, I wanted to get to know you a bit," I began.

"Certainly. What would you like to know?"

"I understand you write true crime."

"That's correct. I included a brief biography with the application I sent you last month."

"Yes, thank you. You were very thorough. It looks as if you meet the basic requirements for leasing a cabin at the retreat, but I'd be interested in knowing why you wanted to join our family."

She looked momentarily confused. "Family?"

"I guess I use the term rather loosely, but the authors who've chosen to make the Turtle Cove Writers' Retreat home have bonded in such a way that it feels as if we've become a family. I think you'd find living at the resort to be very inclusive."

Nicole straightened her posture and leaned forward slightly. "I'm interested in finding lodging on the island while I research a book. It isn't my intention to sign a social contract of either a formal or informal kind."

I was about to inform Ms. Carrington that I didn't think she'd be a good fit for our little group when I noticed something in her eyes that didn't quite mesh with her words or body language. I glanced at Clara, who nodded.

"How about I show you the cabin and then you can decide if you're still interested? If you are, I'll process your application and call you in a day or two."

Nicole rose. "Very well. I would like to see the accommodations."

I stood off to the side while she looked around. I expected she'd take a quick glance at the place but instead took her time, moving around the space slowly, running her hand over the countertops and furniture. She never said a word, but I couldn't help but notice the look of longing evident on her face. Finally, after a good twenty minutes, she paused and looked at me.

"What do you think?" I asked.

"I think it will meet my needs. Thank you for your time. I'll expect to hear from you by the end of the day tomorrow."

With that, she turned and walked out. By the time I'd locked up and we returned to the house, she was gone.

"What did you make of that?" I asked Clara.

"She appears to be extremely rigid and almost free of emotion, but it seems clear she's compensating for strong feelings she chooses not to deal with. Although your conversation was brief, I could pick up both fear and longing from her. She's suffered a personal trauma that has caused her to retreat into her intellect. She feels safe living behind the barriers she's erected, but there's a part of her that yearns for the human contact she won't allow herself."

"I feel bad for her. It must be horrible to have to segregate yourself from those around you. Still, I'm concerned about our group as a whole. I wouldn't want to bring someone in who'll create conflict and drama."

Clara paused before she answered. "My intuition tells me Nicole has a good heart. I believe it might be worth taking a chance on her."

"Okay. I'll process her application. If everything checks out, I'll most likely invite her to join us."

"Wonderful. Did you ever find the tools you needed?"

I shook my head. "No. I never had the chance to ask George about bolt cutters. I'll go now."

"He left while you were showing Nicole the cabin. Is it a large bolt you need to cut?"

"No." I explained about the box Jason had found in the wall of one of the cabins. Clara informed me that she was quite good at picking locks and offered to try. I ran up to my room, got the box, and brought it back down to the sunroom, where Clara was waiting. She was as good as her word; after less than thirty seconds, she had the box open.

Inside were several items, including a stack of letters tied together with a pink ribbon, a photograph of a man and woman both smiling at the camera, and a locket. The letters were addressed to someone named Francine.

"There's no return address," I said, "but the letters were all postmarked between April 1963 and July 1964." I looked at Clara. "That's fifty-plus years ago. Do you think the box has been in the wall for fifty years?"

"I suppose it's possible. I remember you telling me the resort has been in your brother's family for three generations. I suppose he must have been a little boy back then."

"Garrett's fifty-eight, so he would have been five when the last letters were written. I wonder if he knows who the man and woman in the photo are."

"You can ask him, but that was a long time ago and he was just a little boy."

"Yes, but if he knew the couple he might recognize them. Garrett is at the hospital in Charleston for some tests this week. I don't think he'll be back on the island until Saturday. I guess it wouldn't hurt to call him to see if anything about this rings a bell. Do you think we should read the letters to see if we can figure out who they're from?"

"I don't see why not. If we knew who they were from, we might be able to track down the owner of the box."

Based on the content of the letters, it appeared they were written by a soldier stationed overseas during the Vietnam War. The letters were signed by someone named Paul, but I didn't find a last name. It was obvious whoever wrote the letters had gone out of his way not to reveal his exact location or the details of his mission overseas. Still, it seemed apparent he was very much in love with Francine.

"It looks like Paul and Francine were involved in a long-distance love affair," I said to Clara. "I've only had the chance to glance at the first couple of letters, but I noticed a few mentions of someone named Tom. If I had to guess, I'd say he might have been Francine's husband, or at least someone she was committed to in some way." I held up one of the letters. "This mentions Paul's fear of Tom's reaction should he find out about the two of them. He also mentions that Tom will be home within a few short weeks, while he has another six months of active duty. He's concerned about Francine and is counseling her not to let on to Tom any of the details of their affair. I guess we can assume Francine stayed at the resort while her husband was overseas, if that's who Tom was. I wonder why she didn't take her box with her when she left."

"Perhaps the letters were left in the cabin at a later date and Francine wasn't actually staying at the resort during the time she received them. Or she was at the resort when the letters were received and by the time she left Tom was with her and she was afraid he would find the letters. She might have decided to leave the box here until she had the opportunity to retrieve it."

"But she never did. Well, my curiosity has been stoked. I wonder if we can track down Francine after all these years."

"If she's still alive."

"I was planning to head over to Gertie's to ask her about helping me host a Thanksgiving dinner for the gang—to which you're invited, of course. I think I'll take the photo and letters with me. I'm not sure how old Gertie is or how old Francine would be if she's still alive, but maybe she knows someone who might remember her."

"That's a good idea, dear. Let me know what you find out."

******

"Afternoon, Gertie," I said as I walked into the cheery café on the wharf, overlooking the marina.

"Afternoon, suga. Coffee?"

"Please." I slipped onto a stool at the counter.

"You lookin' for some vittles as well?"

"Something light. Maybe a sandwich."

"Ham and cheese?"

"Sure. And a pickle on the side."

"So what can I help you with today?" she asked as she pushed my cup in front of me. "You look like a gal on a mission."

"I have several things I want to talk to you about, actually. The first is Thanksgiving. I'd like to host a dinner, but I don't have any experience tackling a meal of that magnitude."

"So you were hoping ol' Gertie could help?"

"I was hoping you could oversee the whole thing. I'd help, of course. I'd pay you, if you'd like. And you'd of course be invited to attend."

Gertie chucked. "I'd be happy to take charge of your little party. How many are you thinkin'?"

"George and Clara are definitely coming, and I'm pretty sure Alex, Brit, and Victoria will be in town. I plan to ask Jack and I'll probably ask Deputy Savage.

Then there's you and me. Oh, and Meg Collins. I guess that's ten."

"We'll plan for twelve. Every time I've hosted a holiday meal I've ended up pickin' up a stray or two with nowhere else to go."

"Twelve sounds perfect. Do you want to make me a grocery list, or should I just give you some money to buy the groceries?"

"Shoppin' for a meal like this will be a two-person activity. This place is closed on Mondays, so why don't we plan to go together?"

"Okay. I'll put it on my calendar. And thanks, Gertie. There's really no way I could pull this off on my own."

"Once you do a big dinner a time or two, you'll start to get the hang of it. We'll need pies. It's best to bake them the day before. I plan to have the café open until noon on Wednesday for the breakfast crowd, so why don't you come over here after I close up? We can bake them together."

I grinned. "I've never baked a pie before so I'm not sure how much help I'll be, but I'm excited to learn. Hopefully, we'll have Alex's mystery wrapped up in plenty of time to do everything we need to for the holiday."

"You kids got a new mystery?"

I was thirty-eight years old and far from being a kid, but somehow, I loved it when Gertie referred to me that way. I didn't think she was anywhere old enough to be my mother, but every time I was with her I felt cared for and nurtured, just the way I'd always dreamed it could be. My mom wasn't really the nurturing sort, so I'd decided to enjoy the mothering that seemed to come naturally to my Southern friend.

"We're investigating the death of Trey Alderman for a book Alex's writing."

"It's about damn time someone looked at that situation. I told Deputy Savage a year ago that Mortie said that boy was murdered, but he didn't seem inclined to do much about it."

Mortie was the ghost who had lived in Gertie's house for more than thirty years and had, surprisingly, been helpful in solving mysteries in the past.

"Did Mortie have any idea who may have drugged Trey?" I asked.

"He didn't give me a name, if that's what you mean. Mortie isn't all that good at names. But he did say it seemed to him the drugs that were in that boy's drink were intentionally slipped to him so he'd miss the game the next day. 'Course, you need to keep in mind that Mortie doesn't always get things right. He's dead, after all."

"Mortie's theory makes a lot of sense. Anyone who held a grudge against Trey—and it seems he was the sort to attract all sorts of grudges—could very well have wanted to mess up his chance to shine at the charity event." I leaned over the counter and hugged Gertie. "Thanks for the info. I think Mortie might be on to something."

"Glad I could help."

"Now, for my last question. My contractor found a metal box hidden in the wall of one of the cabins this morning. There were letters in it dated more than fifty years ago, along with a locket and a photo." I handed Gertie the latter. "I don't suppose you know who the people in this photo are?"

Gertie took it. "No. I'm afraid this looks as if it's before my time. Did the letters have a name on them?"

"The person who wrote them was a man named Paul who was stationed overseas during Vietnam. The recipient, who I imagine must have been the one to put the letters in the box in the wall, was a woman named Francine. No last names were mentioned, although there were references to a man named Tom, who seemed to be someone Francine was committed to in some way."

"Sounds like you got yourself a juicy mystery. You gonna investigate both this and Trey's death?"

"No," I answered. "While I'm interested in Francine's story and would like to find her if she's still alive, I told Alex I'd help him with his book and that's what I intend to do. Still, I figure it won't take a lot of time to ask around about Francine while I'm investigating Trey's death. Can you think of anyone who was around back then and might remember her now?"

"Have you asked Garrett? He would have been a little kid back then, but if the woman stayed at the resort for any length of time, he might remember something about her."

"He's in the hospital having some tests done and won't be back until Saturday, but I think I'll call him. If he doesn't remember himself, he might have an idea who to ask."

"Let me think on it a bit too. I'm sure I can come up with a few folks who are old enough and have been on the island long enough. Bring me by a copy of the photo so I can show it around."

"Thanks, Gertie. I'll have Jack duplicate it, then bring you a copy. We can talk some more later about Thanksgiving. And if you have anyone you want to invite, feel free."

"Thanks, suga. I just might invite a date, if that's okay."

I raised an eyebrow. "A date?" I'd never known Gertie to even mention a man in a romantic way, past or present.

"New man in town. He's got a right nice look about him."

"Does this new man have a name?"

"He does."

"Are you going to tell me what it is?"

Gertie winked. "Not just yet. As soon as I know if the man is interested in what ol' Gertie has to offer, I'll let you know."

"He'd be a fool not to want what you have to offer, and I have a feeling you wouldn't be lookin' to hook up with a fool."

Lookin' to hook up? Geez, I was beginning to sound like Gertie.

She chuckled. "You got that right, suga."

Chapter 3

Friday, November 17

Thursday had been an odd day between my interview with Nicole Carrington and finding the letters in the box in the wall. I'd called Garrett, who didn't remember anyone named Francine who'd stayed at the resort when he was a child, but he'd said he was happy to look at the photo if I wanted to bring it to the senior home on Saturday. Today I had plans to jump into Alex's investigation. I grabbed a quick bite to eat before heading to the *Gull Island News*.

The fact that a superrich, supersuccessful author would buy a failing newspaper had shocked everyone in the literary world, but after having spent some time with Jack, I could understand why he would walk away from his glamorous life to spend his days in a dingy office running newspapers off an antiquated press. Of course, Jack hadn't given up his old life completely. He did live in an oceanfront mansion and still published a best-selling novel every year; it was just that his life between the novels had evolved from champagne brunches and world travel to working harder than most men did to make a go of an enterprise that was probably doomed from the start.

"Morning Jack," I said, setting a bag of his favorite glazed doughnuts on the counter. "Thanksgiving, the retreat. You in?"

"I'm in. You know how to make a turkey?"

"Nope. I've never tried, which is why I invited Gertie. She's going to steer the ship and I'm going to help. You can bring the wine."

"I know; the good stuff."

"Exactly."

Jack poured me a cup of coffee and set it on the counter in front of me. He even remembered the cream. "So, are you ready to do some sleuthing today?"

I took a sip of my coffee. "I am, but I have two questions I want to ask you first that have nothing to do with the case."

Jack took a huge bite of his doughnut. "Okay; shoot."

"You know we got final clearance for the second three of the cabins we're renovating, right? Victoria took one of them, which leaves me with two. I interviewed someone yesterday who's looking for a short-term rental. While her credit checked out and I've confirmed she's a legitimate writer, I'm hesitant to accept her application because of her personality. I don't like to think of myself as an elitist, but I do feel I have a responsibility to find tenants who'll complement and not hinder the rapport our group has established."

"What's wrong with her personality?" Jack asked.

"She seems really cold, although I had Clara sit in on the interview and she seemed to think the cold exterior is a defense mechanism of some sort. Clara thinks she'll loosen up a bit once she gets to know us, but I'm not so certain. She as much as said she wasn't interested in becoming involved with us socially."

"Is that a deal breaker? As long as she isn't confrontational and doesn't stir up trouble, does it really matter if she wants to keep to herself?"

I thought about Jack's comment. A tenant who kept to herself shouldn't be a problem as long as she wasn't out to cause trouble.

"I guess you're right, and I do feel like I should get the units leased as quickly as possible. Garrett is footing the bill for the renovations and I'm sure the extra income would be welcome."

"Did you ask him about it?"

"I didn't ask him about this person specifically, but we did discuss guidelines for leasing the cabins. Basically, he said I should use my best judgment when it came to making decisions about the resort. I think he wants me to take ownership, if you know what I mean."

"I do. And are you comfortable taking ownership?"

"I'm not sure. I've never owned or even worked for a small business before, and I certainly don't have a background running a resort. I'm not qualified in the least to take charge of the place. I tried to tell that to Garrett, but he just said I had good instincts and would figure it out."

"You do have good instincts. What does your gut tell you about the applicant?"

I paused and thought about it for a minute. I remembered the haunted look in her eye, as well as the look of longing as she walked through the cabin. "I guess I'm willing to give her a try. If she wants to keep to herself, I don't suppose that will negatively affect anyone." I looked at Jack. "Thanks for helping me work through this."

"No problem. I'm always happy to help a friend in need. You said you had two questions…"

"My contractor found a metal box hidden in the wall in one of the cabins yesterday. Inside was a photograph of a young couple, a locket, and a stack of letters." I described the contents of the letters I'd read. "I don't suppose you have any idea how to track down a person with only a first name?"

"Not a clue. It's intriguing. Are you going to investigate?"

"Not formally. At least not now. I promised Alex I'd help him, and he deserves my full attention. Once we wrap up his case, maybe I'll look in to the letters. It's been over fifty years since they were written; a few more weeks until they're returned to their owner can't make all that much difference."

"I agree."

"So, have you found anything new about Alex's case?"

"I have. Trey's death, unlike the last ones we looked in to, occurred recently. That means information about it is more readily available. Add to the fact that Trey died on national television and the result is that there are a lot of news articles to pull from. In some ways, there are almost too many resources. The tricky part is going to be weeding through everything to figure out what's relevant and what's hype."

"But you think you might have found something relevant?"

Jack popped the last of his doughnut into his mouth, chewed, and swallowed before answering. "I think I might have. Hang on and let me get my file."

I took another sip of my coffee while I waited for him to get something from his desk. He'd done a lot to clean the office up, but it could still use a couple of coats of paint and some new furniture. Not that Jack entertained here, but I thought it would get old spending time in a space that was this drab and old-fashioned.

"Okay, here's what I have." He set the folder on the counter between us. First, he pulled out a photo of a man I assumed was Trey, stretched out on home plate with the umpire, his teammates, and a coach surrounding him. Trey had died during a public event, so it made sense there would be tons of photos in circulation at a time when everyone had a camera readily available on their phone.

"What am I looking at?" I asked.

Jack pointed to the photo. "Look over here. In the crowd. See the man in the light blue shirt?"

"Yeah, I see him. Is that someone important?"

"That's Coach Cranston."

I squinted to get a better look at the slightly balding man. "So he went to the game. Alex said all the suspects were there. Is the photo in some way significant?"

"Maybe. Look at the man standing next to him."

I glanced at the tall man with dark hair and a thin frame. "So? Who is he?"

"Jett Strong's father."

I looked at the photo more closely. Both men were looking toward home base, but neither looked particularly shocked.

"Was Jett from this area as well?"

"No. As far as I know, he grew up in the small town in Kansas where his parents still live."

"So Mr. Strong came to Charleston to watch his son play in a televised charity event and he just happened to be standing next to Trey's high school coach at the exact moment Trey died, leaving Jett the sole superstar in college baseball? Seems suspicious."

"I agree." Jack set that photo aside and pulled over another one. "At first I was giving them both the benefit of the doubt. It made sense that they'd be at the game, and in the first photo I found that included them in it, they were standing side by side but not speaking or even looking at each other. It was possible they just happened to be watching the game from the same place. But then I found this." Jack pointed to the second photo again.

"That looks like Jett's dad and Coach Cranston in the parking lot. The sun is still high in the sky, but no one's around, so this was probably taken during the game."

"Very good. When I first saw it, I wasn't aware of when the game was played, but because there aren't any people coming or going, I assumed the photo was taken while the game was going on. They seem to be having an intense conversation. Look at Coach Cranston's jaw. It's as if his entire mouth is clenched. And while Jett's dad is the one doing the talking, look at his focus. His eyes are narrowed and his lips tight. I'd be willing to bet neither of them was aware that someone was taking their photo. The question is, why *was* someone taking their photo? If the game was still going on, Trey was still alive. Nothing had happened yet to cast suspicion on either man. Why would some random passerby take a photo of these particular men?"

"Maybe the person taking the photo wasn't a random passerby. It could have been someone who either knew something was going on between them or suspected it. How did they even know each other?"

Jack frowned. "I don't know. I did some checking and could confirm that Coach Cranston stopped by the party the previous evening. I was also able to verify that Mr. Strong wasn't on the island that night. He flew into Charleston and spent the night in a hotel. As far as I know, Trey didn't tell Coach Cranston he was going to sign with another agent until some point during the week he was home, so it's unlikely these two men would have had the opportunity to seek each other out and hatch a plot. Coach Cranston was involved in the world of baseball and Jett was a top player, so I suppose it's possible they met in the past at some event or game. When we meet with Coach Cranston we can ask him how he knows Jett's dad. If he's guilty of cooking up a plot to keep Trey from playing in the charity game, he'll most likely lie, but if he's innocent of wrongdoing, he won't have any reason not to give us the information."

"Jett didn't sign with Coach Cranston when he went pro, did he?"

"No. He went with a well-known professional, which is exactly what Trey had decided to do. Keep in mind, Jett would have gone pro whether Trey lived or died. I think the difference is that by the time Jett was drafted, he was the biggest thing in college baseball, not the second biggest. It may be a small thing to us, but to those with big egos…"

"Yeah. I know the type. What else did you find?"

Jack set another photo in front of me, this one of a young woman sitting behind a group of girls who were talking and laughing. The girl behind them was alone, and by the look on her face, she was throwing mental daggers at the others.

"Who are we looking at?" I asked.

"The girl sitting alone is Candy Baldwin. The girls who are laughing and talking are Heather Granger, a girl named Portia Sinclair, who was a friend of Heather's, and Rena Madison."

"Rena and Heather were laughing and talking at the party where Trey was most likely drugged?"

"It appears so," Jack confirmed. "All three girls have drinks in their hands and seem to be relaxed and happy. I looked at this photo for a while to see if I could pick up some sort of hidden emotion, but other than Candy, who looks like she's ready to spit nails, I didn't see any sign of tension in their body language."

"Can I take this and show it to Clara? If someone is faking it, she'll know it."

"Yeah. No problem."

"What's going on in this photo?" I picked up the next photo in the pile, of a very pretty young woman speaking to a nice-looking young man.

"That's Quinn Jenkins and Jett Strong. It was taken at the party. Quinn was Parker Wilson's girl and went to the University of South Carolina, while Jett went to Florida State University. I have no reason to believe the two knew each other before the party, but look at the way Quinn has her hand on Jett's chest and is leaning in close as she talks to him."

I considered the photo. Their conversation did appear to be intimate. "Do you think she's trying to pick him up?"

"That was my first thought, but look at this guy here." Jack pointed to a man standing in the background. He seemed to be watching the couple. The look on his face was one of expectation, not anger.

"Okay, who's that?"

"Parker. It would seem if Quinn was trying to pick up Jett, Parker would have been angry. He might even have interrupted their exchange, but he doesn't look mad."

"He doesn't," I agreed. "Maybe Quinn was trying to get Jett to participate in a threesome."

Jack laughed. "I don't think that's it. What I do think might have been going on was that Quinn was trying to get Jett to help her take Trey down a peg."

"By putting something in his drink so he would miss the game," I realized.

"Possibly. Trey missing the game would have benefited both Jett and Parker. Or Quinn might have had a plan to get rid of both Trey *and* Jett, so Parker would really shine. She may be cozying up to Jett so she can slip something into *his* drink."

"But he didn't get sick."

"But that doesn't mean she didn't have a plan to get rid of the two of them that didn't work out."

I looked more closely at the photo. It definitely appeared as if Quinn was coming on to Jett for one reason or another.

"Do you think we might be reading things in to these photos because we know how things turned out?"

"Maybe," Jack admitted.

"Do you have any others?"

He nodded. "A bunch I've pulled off people's social media accounts, but I don't want to take the time to go over all of them now. Maybe you can come to my place for dinner and we can see what we can find then."

I hesitated. It might seem odd, but despite the fact that Jack had been to the resort many times, I'd never been to his home. I'd been on his yacht, but not his home. Going there felt like we'd be taking a step. It was private and intimate. Was I ready for private and intimate?

I tried to sound nonchalant, though I was feeling terrified. "Yeah, okay." I'd pretty much decided I was done acting like a nervous schoolgirl, and I liked Jack and could see us having a relationship. "Tonight?"

"Tonight's good for me. You know I can't cook. Is takeout with a nice bottle of wine okay?"

"Sounds perfect. What time do you want me to be there?"

"I'll pick you up at the resort. Say around six?"

"Six is good."

Jack smiled. "Great. In the meantime, we have a coach, a chef, and a fisherman to talk to."

Chapter 4

Jack and I decided to begin our interviews with Heather Granger. She'd been Trey's girlfriend for four years and, according to what others had said, she'd held a huge grudge against him on the night of the party, though the photo of her chatting with Rena seemed to indicate otherwise.

Heather, with her fiancé, Devon Prowder, were in the process of renovating an abandoned storefront on the commercial fishing wharf that they planned to use for the seafood restaurant they hoped to open in the next couple of months. Jack had called ahead, so Heather knew we were coming. She greeted us with a smile and offered us a soda from her ice chest.

"Thank you so much for agreeing to meet with us," Jack began.

"Are you kidding?" Heather, who was casually dressed and looked happy and relaxed, asked. "There was no way I was going to pass up the opportunity to meet the famous Jackson Jones. I love your books; I've read every one you've ever written."

Jack smiled. "Thank you. I appreciate that."

Heather turned and looked at me. "I understand you're a writer as well."

"I used to be a newspaper reporter, but I'm working on a mystery novel now that's taking forever to finish."

"I'm sure it'll be great. I look forward to reading it once it's published." Heather turned and looked back to Jack. "You said you had some questions for me about Trey?"

He nodded. "If you have a few minutes."

"Why don't we sit outside? Devon and I plan to provide outdoor seating during the warmer months, but for now we have a table and chairs outside for when we take breaks. The view from the end of the wharf is spectacular."

Jack and I followed Heather through the building, which looked to be nearing the final stages in the remodel, and out onto the deck area. Heather was right; the view from the edge of the wharf was great. I had a feeling Devon and Heather were going to have a huge success on their hands.

"So, what can I tell you?" Heather asked.

"I understand you dated Trey all through high school," Jack began.

"Yeah, we were a couple for almost four years. I really loved him and believed we had a future together, but it seemed he had other plans."

"Had you been in touch with Trey during the three and a half years between your breakup and the party you both attended the night before his death?"

Heather nodded. "A few times. His folks still lived on the island when Trey was in college and he came back to visit every now and again. The gang we hung out with in high school was pretty tight, so we ran into each other a few times at parties and other get-togethers. We even saw each other over Christmas break during his junior year, but it didn't work out in the long run."

"How was that for you?" Jack asked.

"Hard. At first it was really hard. I was devastated when Trey first ended things, but time really does heal all wounds, and eventually seeing him when he came to town became easier to deal with. When we got together that Christmas, I guess I hoped it would lead to something permanent, but it didn't. I don't think Trey wanted to be tied down."

Jack took out his small notebook. "Is it okay if I take notes while we chat?"

"Fine by me. I'm not sure I'll have anything noteworthy to say, though. I know there are people who figured I'd be outraged when Trey brought his new girl to the party the night before he died, but they were wrong. After our Christmas fling, I realized we were never going to be together, so I made up my mind to move on. By the time the party came around almost eighteen months later, I was over him. I found Rena to be funny and interesting. We got along just fine, especially when she told me she'd heard a rumor Trey was planning to dump her after they graduated college. I felt like we were kindred spirits in a way."

"So Rena did know Trey was planning to dump her," I confirmed.

"She suspected. I don't think she had any concrete proof, but during the party she overheard something Hudson had said to a bunch of his buddies. Hudson and Trey were tight, and it stood to reason that Trey would have discussed his plans with him."

Jack jotted down a few things while Heather looked on. It seemed she was really starstruck and totally into watching Jack's every move.

"Do you think Rena was angry enough to want to hurt Trey?" Jack eventually asked.

Heather frowned. "She was definitely pissed off, and I don't think she'd been dumped much before that. She's both beautiful and assertive and it seemed like she was used to getting her own way. But was she angry enough to hurt Trey? I think that's doubtful. She did say something about breaking up with him before he could break up with her, and I overheard her saying she was going to get even with him for treating her badly, but she was totally smashed by that time. I don't think she would have carried out her threats. Still, I only just met her, so I guess I can't really say what she was capable of."

Jack paused, then said, "I understand Candy Baldwin was your best friend in high school."

"Was and still is. She married Hudson, so she's Candy Dickerson now. They bought a cute little house over on Elm Street. It's a tiny little thing, but it has character."

"We've been told Candy was extremely upset when Trey broke up with you."

Heather nodded. "She was furious. Candy and I have been besties since kindergarten. When I hurt she hurts and vice versa. She could see how devastated I was, and I know she struggled with the urge to strangle Trey for what he'd done to me. What he'd done to both of us."

"'Us'?" Jack asked.

"Trey and me and Hudson and Candy weren't only best friends; we were best couple friends. We hung out all the time. Candy and I used to talk about buying houses next door to each other with a connecting gate in the fence. We were going to have our kids at the same time and take family vacations together."

"It sounds like a nice plan," Jack said.

"We'd planned the perfect life, although if I'm honest with myself, I guess I knew deep down inside that our dream was never gonna happen. I knew Trey would pursue a career in baseball, so the idea of us having adjoining houses was pretty slim. Still, Candy and I sort of shoved the reality into a corner of our minds, and when Trey broke up with me, he not only ended my dream of a life with him but Candy's dream of this awesome best friend future."

"Did Candy ever forgive Trey?"

Heather shook her head. "No. She hated him until the end. She never could understand why I eventually decided to let it go and get on with my life. Hudson and Candy got married, as I said, but to this day I can see Candy still mourns the life she believes she would have had if Trey and I got married too."

"Was she angry that you and Rena were friendly at the party?" I asked.

Heather scrunched her brows. "I'm not sure I'd say she was angry, but she hated Rena on sight, so maybe. I remember Candy acting sullen and moody the entire evening. I just wanted to focus on having fun and hanging out with my friends. I won't go so far as to say we had a fight that night, but we were somewhat on the outs. She just seemed intent on bringing me down and I wanted to have fun."

"Did both of you go to the baseball game in Charleston the next day?" I asked.

Heather's smile faded. "Yeah, we were there. That had to be one of the worst days of my life. I think I died a little when Trey didn't get up and I realized he was gone. Things may not have gone as I'd hoped, but we were together for years. Important years. He was and will always be a part of me. I love Devon and I'm very happy to be building a life with him, but I still think of Trey almost every day." Heather looked at Jack. "The medical examiner told Trey's parents his death was an accident. Do you think differently? Is that why you're asking these questions?"

"We're looking in to the possibility that Trey may have been slipped the drugs that led to his death, although at this point it's just a theory."

"That actually makes sense. Trey was an athlete. He took care of his body. I know he drank sometimes, but I'd be very surprised to hear he'd taken drugs voluntarily. Especially the night before a big game. The whole thing never seemed right to me."

"Can you think of anyone at the party who might have been motivated to prevent Trey from playing in the game, or perhaps simply wanted to get back at him for some reason?"

Heather considered Jack's question. "Drugging a guy is pretty serious business. I know Trey ruffled some feathers, and there were people at the party who thought he was a jerk. We've already said Rena and Candy were angry with him, but I don't see either one killing him. I saw him arguing with Coach Cranston that night, but the coach is a nice guy who really cares about his boys, so I can't see him intentionally hurting one of them."

Heather tapped her chin as she continued to think. "There was a guy there named Jett. I'd never met him before; he wasn't from the island. I'm not sure why he was even at the party unless he came with Trey, although they didn't seem to be getting along all that well, so it would be odd if Trey invited him. I heard he played for a rival college, so he and Trey must have known each other. Wouldn't it be strange to invite a competitor to a party in your hometown? Still, if Trey didn't invite him, I don't know who did."

"What about Coach Cranston?" I asked.

"Why would Coach Cranston invite some guy he didn't even know to a party?"

"Trey had recently told the coach he was looking elsewhere for an agent. Maybe Coach Cranston was hoping to sign Jett in his place."

"Maybe," Heather said, although she looked doubtful.

"I understand Dexter Parkway was at the party," Jack said.

"Dex? You can't think Dex would hurt Trey. Dex idolized Trey."

"Yes, but I have to wonder if Dexter continued to have fond feelings for a man who'd treated him like a second-class citizen when they were in high school. He was a senior in college by that time and I understand he's quite brilliant. It wouldn't be surprising if he'd started to look at things differently once he came into his own."

"You're totally off with that one. Dex is a pussycat. He would never hurt anyone. In fact, I can't think of a single person at the party who…" Heather stopped speaking abruptly.

"Did you remember something?" Jack asked.

"No," she said as a tear slipped down her cheek. "It's nothing. It just hit me that someone might actually have murdered Trey. He could be a jerk, but he didn't deserve that. He was self-centered, but he could also be sweet and thoughtful. I really did love him. In some ways, I always will."

Jack closed his notebook, then placed a hand on Heather's arm. "I'm sorry we had to ask such painful questions."

She wiped away a tear. "That's okay. I can usually talk about Trey without falling apart, but this conversation brought back some memories of happier times."

I could see Jack felt awkward about having made Heather cry because he changed the subject and chatted with her for a few minutes about his upcoming book. That seemed to lighten her mood considerably. When he went to his car to find a book in the trunk and signed it for her, you would have thought she'd won the lottery. I guess most of the time I forgot how popular he and his books were to so many people. As I watched him charm Heather, I realized being *on* all the time must be incredibly exhausting. For the first time, I understood why Jack would want to run away to Gull Island, where most of the time he could be just Jack.

"It was nice of you to autograph a book for Heather. I could see it meant a lot to her."

He shrugged. "It was no big deal. I'm asked to sign books all the time. Do you want to grab some lunch before we head to the high school to speak to Coach Cranston? I don't think he'll be available for another hour."

"I am hungry. There's that new sandwich shop just down the street. They have an outdoor patio and it's a nice day."

"Sounds perfect," Jack said as he turned the car in that direction.

We placed our order, then found a place to sit. The patio was surrounded by a large garden that would be lovely most of the year but was mostly dormant in late fall.

"So, what did you think about what Heather had to say?" I asked Jack.

"I believe she cared for Trey and would never have hurt him, but I also think she's hiding something. She said her tears were because our conversation brought up memories, but the timing told me something had suddenly occurred to her. Something painful. Something she wasn't ready to talk about."

"I agree. She must be protecting someone. I'm just not sure who."

We fell silent as we ate our lunch. I'm sure my sandwich was delicious, but I could have been eating cardboard for all the attention I paid to it. I was anxious to speak to Coach Cranston. If he'd invested time and money in Trey's career only to be pushed out just because things were beginning to happen for Trey, he must have become furious at the young man many had indicated he thought of as a son. I wasn't certain where our interview with him would lead, but I was eager to find out. I'd never met him, but Jack knew him because he reported on Gull Island's sports scene as well as its news. I'd be taking notes while Jack conducted the interview.

Gull Island High School was small, with a modest enrollment, as were many of the others scattered among the islands. The fact that any athlete from a tiny school would receive national attention was a testament to how good Trey really was. Not only had the team gone undefeated during his reign as baseball king, but, based on what I'd heard, it had not only beaten its competition but massacred them. In the years since Trey had graduated, the team was mediocre at best.

Coach Cranston was in his office working on paperwork when we arrived. He greeted Jack with a hearty handshake, and they chatted about high school sports for a few minutes before we began the interview. Up to this point I'd been thinking the coach was our strongest suspect, but he seemed so relaxed and open with Jack, I found myself reexamining my assumptions.

"You said on the phone you wanted to talk about Trey Alderman," Coach Cranston said.

"I'm helping a colleague who's writing a book about his baseball career with some research. I know you're busy, so I'll try to be brief."

"I'm always happy to talk about Trey. That boy single-handedly put Gull Island High on the map. What do you want to know?"

Jack started off by asking about Trey's background at the school and the games he played in. I considered this a soft approach, but under the circumstances, easing into the difficult questions probably was best. I listened as Coach Cranston shared memories of shutout games and game-winning home runs. It didn't seem as if he held a grudge, but

Jack hadn't worked around to the tougher questions yet.

"Did you stay in touch with Trey after he went off to college?" he asked.

"I did. That boy was like a son to me. I went to as many of his games as I could manage and we always shared a meal when I was in town. It about killed me when he died." Coach Cranston looked down at his desk. I could see he was taking a moment to get his emotions under control.

"Were you at the game where he suffered his heart attack?" Jack asked. He knew the answer but must be looking for the coach's reaction.

"I was there. You know, I almost didn't go. Trey was a great kid, but we'd a falling-out just before that game. He'd made a decision he felt was best for his career, but at the time I felt slighted and was angry at him. We'd argued the night before and my emotions were still pretty raw, but in the end, I knew I would regret it if I wasn't there, so I went."

Jack shifted in his chair. "I understand the two of you had discussed the possibility of you acting as his agent when he went pro."

Coach Cranston nodded. "That was the plan. We talked about it often. But in the end, he decided to go with a professional. As I said, my feelings were hurt, but after I thought it over, I realized he was right. Trey had a brilliant career ahead of him. He needed a brilliant agent with a proven track record. It was such a shame he never had the opportunity to fulfill his potential."

"Did you consider acting as agent for any other young baseball players?"

The coach shook his head. "Naw. Trey was special. I wanted to be a part of that. I'm pretty happy here, coaching my kids."

"There's a theory floating around that someone spiked Trey's drink with the drugs that led to his death and his heart attack wasn't accidental at all."

Coach Cranston pursed his lips. "I've always wondered about that. Trey wasn't the type to use drugs. It was totally out of character for him, especially before a big game. He did seem different that week, though."

"Different how?"

Cranston drummed his fingers on his desk before he answered. "Angsty. Like he had something heavy on his mind. The conversation he had with me couldn't have been an easy one for him, and I didn't take it all that well at first. But I think there was more going on than that. He seemed distracted and somewhat worried."

"I heard he planned to break up with his girl," I said. "Could it have been that?"

"Doubtful. Trey had his eye on the Baseball Hall of Fame. He wasn't going to let some girl slow him down. No, if he was worried about something, I'd be willing to bet it had something to do with baseball."

"The draft was right around the corner," Jack offered. "I suppose he could have been worried about how that would work out."

"Perhaps."

"I understand Jett Strong, Trey's biggest rival for the top spot in college baseball, was not only involved in the game in which he died but was on the island before the game as well," I added to move things along.

"Yup, that's right. Jett was invited to play in the game, same as Trey. I don't think the two of them were friends, but I do remember him being at the party to welcome Trey home the night before the game."

"Were they getting along at the party?" I asked.

"Don't rightly know. I was there, but I didn't stay long. Things were awkward between us after we had our talk."

"I've been told Jett's father was also at the game. What can you tell me about him?" Jack asked.

"Not much. I don't know him, though I'm aware he's very involved in his son's career. He has a reputation for being ruthless when it comes to getting for Jett what he thinks he deserves. I heard he hired a series of private coaches for Jett during his high school and even college years, but none ever lasted long. Apparently, Mr. Strong has a reputation for firing anyone who disagrees with him about any aspect of his son's career."

"Did you speak to Mr. Strong at the game?" I asked.

Coach Cranston shook his head. "Nope. Not that I recall." He looked up at the wall clock. "Sorry to cut this short, but I have to teach a physical education class in about ten minutes."

"No problem. We were about done anyway." Jack stood and held out his hand. "Thank you for taking the time to speak to us. You've been very helpful."

We walked in silence back to Jack's car. After we'd both gotten in I turned to him and asked if he thought Coach Cranston was lying about not having spoken to Jett's dad.

"Yeah, I think he might have been lying. I can't believe he'd have a conversation as intense as the one we saw in the photo and not recall having it a year and a half later."

"Should we confront him with the photo?"

"I think we might want to let Deputy Savage handle that. I have a copy of the photo with me. Let's stop by to see what he thinks. I'm afraid if you and I confront him, he'll just clam up, but he might talk to Savage, especially if he really doesn't have anything to hide."

"I agree. Both Coach Cranston and Deputy Savage have lived on the island a long time. I imagine they know each other well. It stands to reason Cranston might be more open to sharing his thoughts and memories with someone he knows and trusts."

Chapter 5

Luckily, Rick Savage was in his office. There was a time I would have doubted his willingness to speak with us, but our relationships had developed over the past few months and most of the time I considered him to be an ally. It was true that almost everything he said to us was prefaced with an insistence that the information was off the record, but he'd been instrumental in helping us with the last couple of cases we'd researched, and I hoped he'd be willing to participate in this investigation as well. Alex had brought up the idea of investigating the death of Trey Alderman at our Halloween dinner, and at the time, Rick had hinted he would be willing to work with us if no laws were broken or crimes covered up.

"I was wondering when the two of you would show up," Deputy Savage said when we walked into his office. "I take it you've begun the investigation you discussed at Halloween."

"We have," I said as I slid into one of the chairs on the far side of his desk. "We've only just begun, but we already have something for you to do."

Savage chuckled. "You don't say. And what do you have in mind?"

Jack shared our conversation with Coach Cranston and then showed him the photo of the coach arguing with Jett's dad. "We figured maybe you could follow up with him."

The deputy looked at the photo. "The problem is, I'm not officially investigating this case. Questioning the coach in an official capacity when the case has already been closed isn't going to go over well with the new sheriff. As crazy as it seems, he has the idea that I should spend my time investigating open cases."

"What would it take to reopen this case?" I asked.

"Something concrete that would prove Trey Alderman's death wasn't accidental, as the original investigator determined. And keep in mind the case was never open in our county. Trey died in Charleston and it was the Charleston PD who looked in to his death and made the determination that it was an accident."

I sat back in my seat. "Okay; if you can't help us in an official capacity, can you help us behind the scenes?"

"It depends on what you want me to do."

"Can you get hold of the report that was filed after the original investigation?"

Savage hesitated. "I'm sure I could. I'm not sure I should share it with you, however."

"So don't share it. Just get it and look it over. If there's something you feel we should know as we proceed, you can slip it into casual conversation."

Deputy Savage steepled his fingers as he considered my request. "I suppose it wouldn't be a bad idea for me to look at the report. I probably should have back then, although at the time no one was suggesting that Trey's death might have been anything *but* an accident."

I smiled. "Great. And if you see something you think might help us, you can casually let us know. By the way, I'm giving a Thanksgiving dinner. You're invited, if you aren't busy."

Deputy Savage looked surprised by the invitation. "Can I let you know in a day or two? I appreciate the invite, but I should check with my brother to make sure he hasn't made plans that include me."

"That'll be fine." I stood up. "And thank you for the other. We look forward to chatting with you once you've had a chance to read the report."

Jack and I headed back to his car, discussing our next move. It seemed the best thing to do now was to get everything we'd learned so far onto the whiteboards while our interviews were fresh in our minds. I wanted to pick up my car, which I'd left at the newspaper, so we headed in that direction.

"Let's grab the rest of your photos as well. We can look through them and post comments on the whiteboard for any that seem relevant. We may even want to make copies and hang those we feel are most significant. It'd be good to get input from the others.

"I have copies on my computer, so we can do that," Jack agreed.

"It's really bothering me that Coach Cranston seems to be lying about having spoken to Jett's dad at the game," I commented. "You don't think he's actually guilty of conspiring to kill Trey, do you?"

"Kill him, no. But if the intention was simply to cause him to miss the game, maybe. I hope not, but he'd just been burned, and obviously Mr. Strong had a vested interest in having his son shine during a televised event so close to the draft. I could almost imagine a situation where Coach Cranston called Jett's dad to let him know he was available, should Jett need an agent. The two of them might have chatted and, during the conversation, hatched a plan to make sure Trey was in no shape to play. It bothers me that the coach showed up at a party where the average age was probably twenty-two. Especially because he'd so recently been burned by Trey."

"Yeah, it does seem odd, unless he was there to spike his drink."

"I like the guy. He genuinely seems to care about the kids he coaches and the community as a whole. I really hope he's innocent, but if we're beginning to create a suspect list, I think we'd be remiss not to include him."

"Agreed. Let's create three lists: suspect, maybe a suspect, and not a suspect right away, so we're grouping people from the beginning. We can always move them around as new information becomes available."

At the resort, we found George and Clara in the dining area sharing a pot of tea. They were happy to help us, so we spread the photos out on the table and began recording our impressions on a whiteboard.

We started by making the three lists. Coach Cranston went on the suspect list, Heather on the not-a-suspect one. Those were the only two people we'd spoken to so far, so they were the only ones we recorded. Then we talked about the fact that while we didn't think Heather would try to hurt Trey, we suspected she was hiding something; we made a note to follow up on that.

"What do you make of this photo?" I asked Clara as I handed her the one of Candy glaring at Heather while she chatted with Rena.

She took the photo and focused her attention on it. I could see she was taking a really good look at the details, which should increase her chances of getting a successful reading.

"The girl sitting in the back watching the others is scared."

"Scared?" I asked. I'd picked up anger, not fright.

"She knows something the others don't. This knowledge is a burden and she's unsure how to proceed. I sense she's conflicted about the secret she's been burdened with."

I looked at Jack. "Maybe she knew someone had or was planning to drug Trey."

"Maybe. Should we add her to the suspect list?"

"Let's wait to add anyone else until after we speak to them. Though I feel like she'll end up being a suspect." I turned back to Clara. "What else do you see?"

"The girl on the left isn't as relaxed as she appears to be. See how she's gripping the cup she's holding?"

I looked at Heather's hand. She *did* seem to be holding it a lot more tightly than necessary, now that I took a closer look.

"And this girl here." Clara pointed to Portia Sinclair. "She's pretending to be involved in the conversation the girls around her are having, but she's actually looking over Heather's shoulder."

Again, I looked more carefully at the photo. It seemed as if Portia was interacting with the others, but upon closer examination, her eyes did seem to be focused on something in the distance. "I wonder if we should add her to the list of people to interview. Do we know if she still lives on the island?"

"I don't know," Jack answered. "But I'll add her to the list and find out."

I turned back to Clara and pointed to Rena. "What about this girl? Can you tell what's going on with her?"

"She has a look of confidence. Of satisfaction. She reminds me of the cat who's spotted the bird and is just waiting for the right time to dine on it. She doesn't display the same telltale ticks as the others. She looks as if she's enjoying herself. If I had to choose one of the four to be most cautious of, it would be her. The situation the girls have found themselves in is one that should be uncomfortable and awkward. It's not natural for Trey's current girlfriend to be quite so comfortable with his ex. She's either a sociopath or she honestly doesn't care what happens next."

I glanced at Jack. He was frowning, but I could see he was mulling over everything Clara had said. When Clara was on, she was really *on*, and as I examined the photo again, I sensed she was definitely on today.

"What about this photo?" I pushed the one of Coach Cranston talking to Jett's dad in front of her.

She picked it up and looked at it. "These men are involved in an intense conversation, but I'm not picking up on anything unusual. The eyes behind the photo, however, are another thing entirely."

"The eyes behind the photo? You mean the photographer?"

"Exactly. I sense rage. If I had to guess, I'd say the photographer is taking the photos to prove a point or tell a story. He might be the killer, or he might know who the killer is."

I turned to Jack. "Where did you get this photo?"

He shrugged. "I'm not sure offhand. Some of the photos were from the social media pages of people who knew Trey; others I acquired by doing Google searches for things relating to Trey and the charity game." Jack picked up the photo. "I'm pretty sure this was posted to a board in a chat room. I'm sure I saved the information on my computer. I'll check when I get back to the office."

I glanced back at Clara. "I don't want to tire you out, but I'm going to leave these photos here. If you wouldn't mind looking through them when you have time, that would be great. If you find anything of significance, let me know."

"Of course, dear. I'd be happy to."

I glanced at Blackbeard, who was sitting on his perch watching us. He hadn't said a word for more than two days, which was completely out of character for him. I hoped he was feeling all right. Of course, I didn't know a thing about caring for a bird or recognizing the signs of a problem. I'd have to ask Garrett about that the next time Blackbeard and I visited him. I should take him with me the next day, when I planned to show Garrett the photo I'd found in the box in the wall. I wanted to see if Garrett felt up to joining us on Thanksgiving as well.

"Any thoughts?" I asked the bird, who was watching Jack as he wrote on the whiteboard.

He looked from Jack to me, then back to Jack, but didn't respond.

"Are you feeling okay?"

Still no response.

I looked at George and Clara. "Have either of you heard Blackbeard say anything today?"

Both confirmed they hadn't.

"I wonder if I should call Garrett. I hate to worry him, but I don't know a thing about sick birds."

"I know what veterinarian Garrett took him to," George volunteered. "I can go with you if you want to take him in for a look."

I glanced at Jack. "Maybe I should. Can I call you later?"

"Sure. I have some work to do anyway. Call me when you get back."

******

The Gull Island Veterinary Hospital was run by a nice woman named Kelly Fisher. She'd taken care of Blackbeard when Garrett first had his stroke, so she knew him well. I hoped she'd have a sense of whether his behavior was within the realm of normal; not only was she a doctor but she'd known him a lot longer than I had.

"Blackbeard, it's so good to see you," Kelly greeted him. The vet turned to me. "You must be Garrett's sister."

"Jill Hanford. I'm happy to meet you."

"So, what's the problem with this handsome boy?"

"As you probably know, I've taken over his care because Garrett isn't able to have him at the senior home. To be honest, I don't know a thing about birds. Garrett gave me a few instructions—what to feed him and what foods to avoid and that sort of thing—but I have no idea what sort of behaviors to be concerned about."

Kelly held out her arm and Blackbeard flew onto it. "What exactly is it that he's done that you're concerned about?"

"He isn't talking. No one has heard him say a word in several days and he's usually such a chatterbox."

"Is he eating and drinking?"

I nodded. "He seems to be."

Kelly offered me a soft smile. "I wouldn't worry. Blackbeard will say something when he has something to say. As long as you're here, though, I'd like to give him a checkup."

"That would be great." I sighed with relief.

"You can wait in the reception area if you'd like. I won't be long."

I called Garrett while I waited. He assured me that while it was uncharacteristic for Blackbeard not to speak, it wasn't necessarily a sign that he was sick. He said Kelly was an excellent vet; if she gave him a clean bill of health, there was nothing to worry about. While I had him on the line, I informed him that I'd bring Blackbeard by to see him the following afternoon.

******

I headed upstairs to get ready for my date with Jack when I returned from the vet's. After taking a quick shower, I stood in front of the open closet in my bra and underwear, deciding what to wear. Jack had asked me to come to his home so we could look at more of the photos he'd found and discuss the case; I supposed technically this was more of a business meeting than a date, so a dress seemed a bit much. On the other hand, jeans and a sweatshirt, my usual kick-around-the-house attire, seemed too casual for my first foray into Jack's private space.

"Jill, are you in there?" Vikki called from the other side of the door.

"Yeah. Come in," I called back.

Vikki entered the room and sat down on the side of the bed. "Are you going out?"

"Dinner at Jack's house to discuss the case."

"Jack's house." Vikki raised an eyebrow. "Sounds intimate."

I glanced at Vikki, whose grin clearly communicated that she thought there was more going on than there actually was. "Not intimate; just business. Still, I can't decide what to wear. A dress doesn't seem right for a working dinner, but jeans and a sweatshirt don't feel right either."

Vikki got up and joined me in front of the closet. She sorted through hangers for a minute before selecting a sweater that fell to my midthigh. It was soft and hugged my frame nicely, and the rich cinnamon color was perfect for an autumn evening.

"Try this," Vikki said, "with your black leggings and dark brown boots."

She was right; the outfit was perfect. "Thanks. I should have asked you in the first place. You always know the right thing to wear."

"Wear, maybe. Do, not necessarily."

I pulled the sweater over my head before rummaging around in my dresser for the pair of leggings. "What do you mean by that?" I asked.

Vikki sighed. "Rick asked me out to dinner. I want to go, but I don't know if I should. You remember what happened the last time."

I did remember. Rick and Vikki's first date had turned into a night of passion so intense that love-'em-and-leave-'em Victoria Vance had been unable to handle the depth of her emotions and ended up leaving his house in the middle of the night, only to end up in another man's bed.

"I know your first date with Rick was a lot more intense than you're comfortable with, but that doesn't mean your second date has to end up the same way. It's fine to slow things down. Go to dinner. Reconnect. Keep it casual, and whatever you do, don't go back to his house."

"Easier said than done." Vikki groaned. "There's something about that man that makes me want to undress him every time I see him. He's so sweet and kind, but he's also rugged, with a look in his eye that lets you know that if pushed, he can be just a little dangerous as well. And his body…what can I say? He's gorgeous."

"He is put-together rather nicely," I agreed as I slipped on the leggings. "But if you want to have a relationship with him—a real relationship, not just sex—you need to let him in."

Vikki fell back onto the bed so she was staring at the ceiling. "I know. You're right. We should slow things down. I do want to see if we can have something together and I know I'll have to allow him in emotionally if I want to do that, but I'm scared."

"Of what?" I asked.

Vikki paused. She sat up and looked at me. "I don't know. Falling in love. Being hurt. Losing the part of me that makes me who I am. Sex is easy when it isn't all wrapped up in deep emotions, but when you really care about the person you're with, it gets complicated."

"Complicated isn't always bad," I reminded her.

Vikki laughed. "Look who's talking. You have this great guy who wants to date you—I mean really *date* you—and even though I can see you're totally in to him, you continue to resist him at every turn. Why exactly is *that*?"

I frowned but didn't answer. Vikki had a point. I knew Jack would like to explore the idea of our becoming intimate, and while I cared for him deeply, I blocked his every attempt to expand the parameters of our relationship beyond that of casual friendship. In the beginning, it had seemed I had valid reasons for doing that, but I'd totally forgotten what they were.

"Look, you don't have to answer," Vikki said. "We're both messes, just in different ways. The reason I came in here in the first place was because Clara told me about the letters you found. The romantic within me was more than a little intrigued."

I handed Vikki the box with the letters, photo, and locket. "Jack will be here any minute, but feel free to look at all this. Maybe we can talk about it tomorrow. I'm trying very hard not to get distracted by this mystery because I promised Alex I'd help him."

"I don't have a lot to do regarding Alex's case. Maybe I can work on this a bit. We'll chat tomorrow. Tonight, just try to relax and enjoy your dinner with this great guy who really seems to care about you."

"Okay." I hugged Vikki. "I'll talk to you tomorrow."

******

I knew Jack's house would be amazing, but even with my high expectations, I wasn't prepared for how truly awesome it was. Not only was it huge, but it was laid out ranch style on top of a wide bluff overlooking the ocean.

"It looks like you've been working on the case," I said as I noticed a pile of file folders on the dining table.

"I've been setting up interviews for tomorrow. Will you be available in the morning? I thought maybe we'd try to speak to Hudson and Candy Dickerson next."

I nodded. "Yeah, I can be available. I'm taking Blackbeard to see Garrett, but we aren't going until two. Are you planning to speak to them together or separately?"

"I'm hoping separately. I called and spoke to Hudson today. He said if I came by the marina around nine he'd be available to answer any questions I have. His boat is down for repair, so he's leaving to visit a friend at around ten."

"I can be ready. Do you want to pick me up at eight-thirty?"

"That'll work. I still need to nail down a time to speak to Candy. She's working at the market these days, but when I spoke to her earlier she said I could come by on her break. She's going to text me in the morning to let me know what time that will be, though she said she's usually off in the late morning."

"Sounds fine to me." I picked up a folder and thumbed through it. "I'm anxious to hear what they have to say."

"Me too." Jack took the folder from my hand and set it back onto the table. "But tonight isn't about working the case. Tonight is about us getting to know each other a little better."

"It is?" Suddenly, my heart started to pound and my legs began to shake ever so slightly. I wanted to argue that the whole reason I was there was to work the case, but I remembered Vikki's words of advice.

"It is." Jack took my hand and led me out onto the deck, which had been built on the other side of a wall of windows that seamlessly separated the indoor and outdoor living areas. He offered me a glass of wine as I settled into the soft folds of the outdoor sofa. He sat down next to me, close enough that I could feel the heat from his body. I found I rather liked it.

"This view is spectacular," I said after a moment. "If I lived here, I'm not sure I'd ever leave."

"Your own home has a pretty spectacular view," Jack pointed out.

"True. I guess any view, no matter how amazing, becomes part of your everyday scenery after a while. How long have you lived here?"

"Just over a year. I love the view and I have a lot of privacy, but it's occurred to me that the house may be a tad big for just one person. I've actually been kicking around the idea of selling it and looking for something smaller."

I could see how living in such a huge house all by yourself might get lonely at times. I'd lived alone in a series of tiny apartments for much of my adult life, but now I found I enjoyed living at the resort as part of a family. "If you ever get tired of all this space, I have cabins available," I teased.

Jack turned and looked me in the eye, his gaze quite serious. "Thanks. I may take you up on that one day."

"I was kidding. I'm sure you wouldn't want to downsize quite that much. The cabins only have one bedroom."

Jack shrugged. "I was quite serious. This house is amazing, but it's just a house, and one I don't spend very much time in. The cabins at the resort might be small, but you've created something exceptional at Turtle Cove. You've created a family. At times, I envy that you have people to go home to at the end of the day."

I wasn't sure what to say to that, so I didn't say anything at all. I leaned back against the sofa and let myself enjoy the perfection of the moment. The sun was setting in the distance, the wine was delicious, and the music Jack had on in the background provided a setting designed for romance. I thought about my conversation with Vikki and wondered if she wasn't right and the time had come to allow Jack in. I wasn't sure we necessarily had a future. In my mind, we were both enjoying a temporary break from our real lives, and I had no reason to believe one or both of us wouldn't eventually decide to return to what we'd left behind. What I did know was that I felt attracted to a man who seemed to be attracted to me in return, and not embracing this time we could have together seemed like such a waste.

"What do you have planned for dinner?" I asked after coming to that decision.

"I picked up some Chinese food, which I'll reheat when we're ready. Are you hungry?"

"Not really. Are you?"

Jack shrugged. "I could wait a bit."

I stood up and held out my hand to him. "Great. Then how about a tour of the house before dinner?"

Jack looked surprised but stood up and took my hand. "Okay, if you'd like. Is there anything specific you'd like to see? It's a big house."

I leaned in and kissed Jack on the neck. "How about we start with your bedroom and take it from there?"

Chapter 6

Saturday, November 18

I woke with a smile on my face. Last night had been the most perfect of my life. Jack and I had made love and then we'd gone into the kitchen together to heat up the Chinese food, barely eating half of it before we'd abandoned our meal to make love again. Jack had wanted me to stay over, but I needed time to process everything, so I told him that I preferred to go home to be ready for our sleuthing date the following morning. Jack being the intuitive guy he is, graciously drove me home and left me at my front door with a very sweet kiss that lingered in my mind as I drifted off to sleep.

My instinct in this situation was to obsess about what the change in our relationship would mean, but I made up my mind to trust Jack to know me well enough to realize I would need a little distance to get used to things. When he picked me up, he seemed happy and relaxed and greeted me with a tall cup of coffee and a very sisterly kiss on the cheek.

"Thank you," I said as he handed me my coffee.

Jack winked. "Can't have my co-sleuth sleeping on the job."

I grinned. "I did have a bit of a late night last evening."

Jack brushed my hand with his as he helped me into his car. "I don't suppose you might be up for another late evening tonight?"

I turned to look at him after buckling my seat belt. "I might."

Jack glanced at me out of the corner of his eye as he put the key in the ignition and started the engine. While Jack tried to blend into the Gull Island lifestyle and tended to dress casually and dine in local establishments, it was apparent by the brand-new Maserati he'd bought just a few weeks ago, he drew the line at living a middle-class lifestyle when it came to his car. Well, there was his mansion as well; while he'd expressed his interest in selling the lavish home, I had a feeling the car was here to stay.

"Did you confirm with Hudson and Candy?" I asked as we sped toward the marina.

He nodded. "We'll meet with Hudson at nine and Candy at eleven. If we have time between, we can grab a bite to eat."

I hung on to my seat as Jack zipped around a corner. "Do you have any idea what sort of approach we should take with them? They were close to both Trey and Heather. It seems they could have a lot of insight into what happened, but they could also feel the need to protect what they know." I glanced at Jack's hands on the steering wheel. They were strong and tanned and I found myself blushing as I remembered them on my body the night before.

"I think we do what we've done in the past," Jack answered. "We take it easy in the beginning and see where the conversation takes us. I know there's a time for the direct approach, but Trey's death is still fairly fresh in everyone's mind, so I think we're likely to get more information with sympathy than confrontation."

"I'm sure you're right."

Jack glanced at me and smiled. I was smiling back as he turned into the marina parking lot. I realized in that moment that if we weren't careful, everyone was going to know how our dinner had gone the previous evening, and for reasons I couldn't quite define, I wasn't ready to share our new relationship status with anyone quite yet.

Hudson Dickerson was a tall man with broad shoulders who looked like he could have had a career in football if he'd wanted one. He had longish brown hair that stuck out from beneath his baseball cap and a smudge of grease on his cheek, which I assumed came from the engine he'd been working on. He seemed friendly enough, greeting us with a smile and offering us cups of coffee so thick I was sure we'd have to chew it to get it down.

He motioned us to seats on one of the benches near where he was working. I found myself glad I wasn't wearing white; the bench looked to be almost as greasy as the engine.

"You wanted to talk to me about Trey?" he asked at last.

"Yes, we do," Jack confirmed. "A friend of ours is writing a book about his life and death, focusing on his baseball career. We're helping him to gather information pertaining to the last weeks before his death."

"His kin know you're doing this?"

"Yes," Jack assured him. "Feel free to call them if you like."

Hudson shrugged. "Don't see why you'd lie. What do you want to know?"

Jack started out slowly, asking him about his relationship with Trey and the years they'd spent together, growing up as best friends. He asked about the Little League teams they'd both played on and the trouble they'd gotten into when left to their own devices over summer vacations. It was obvious Hudson had cared very much about Trey and the conversation wasn't easy for him, but I sensed he'd begun to relax and even begun to trust Jack by the time he got to the more difficult questions about his death.

"What can you tell me about the party?" Jack asked.

"What do you mean? Like who was there and stuff?" Hudson asked.

"Sure. Who was there, who was getting along, who wasn't?"

"Me and a couple of the other guys we went to high school with were the ones who decided to throw the party to celebrate Trey's success. It seemed likely he was going to be drafted into the Major League, and we were all proud of him and the recognition he brought to our high school. Most of the people we invited knew him from before he went to college, but he brought his girl with him, and there were a couple of friends of his I didn't really know."

Jack narrowed his gaze. "I know his girlfriend at the time was named Rena Madison. Were the friends you referred to Jett Strong and Parker Wilson?"

"I don't think Jett was a friend of Trey's. In fact, Jett and Trey seemed to have a pretty fierce rivalry going on. But Rena was his girlfriend, and she invited her friend, Quinn, and Quinn's boyfriend, Parker. I sort of got the idea Parker and Trey weren't all that close, but I didn't sense the hostility I did between Trey and Jett."

"So you think Quinn came to the party as a friend of Rena's and Parker came as Quinn's date?"

"That would be my take on things. Trey had words with Rena about inviting them, but she basically told him that they were her friends and she'd invite them if she wanted to. I don't know if this was widely known, but Trey planned to dump Rena after they got back to college, and it seemed to me that Rena might have somehow gotten wind of that and decided to bring reinforcements to the party."

"And how did Heather take it when Rena showed up?"

"Heather was pissed at first, but I told her what Trey had told me about breaking up with her, and Heather felt sorry for the bitch. I couldn't believe how friendly she was being, although I guess that helped Trey out because Rena basically ignored him once Heather introduced her around a bit."

"I understand Coach Cranston showed up at the party as well."

Hudson nodded. "That was pretty weird. Trey had told him he was going with another agent a couple of days before, and everyone knew Cranston was royally pissed off. I'm not sure why he came, unless it was to meet Jett."

"Jett?"

"Yeah. I saw the two of them talking. They seemed to be cooking something up, but I'm not sure what. Cranston didn't stay long and I didn't notice that he ever approached Trey, but then again, I wasn't watching him, so I suppose they might have talked. I was just glad there wasn't some big confrontation between them. When I saw the coach come in, I was afraid they might end up in a fight. They both tended to use their fists when they were mad."

Jack sat back and crossed his legs. "So you're saying Coach Cranston hit his players?"

"No. Not his players. But Trey wasn't his player anymore. He was an adult, so I'm assuming he'd be fair game in Cranston's eyes."

"Does Cranston have a history of violence?" Jack asked.

Hudson shrugged. "Sure, I guess. Or at least he did. I heard he had to take anger management classes after he got into a scuffle with another coach in a bar and had a bit too much to drink."

"There's a theory out there that Trey's drink was spiked without his knowledge at the party and didn't intend to take the drugs that eventually led to his death."

"Oh, that's a fact," Hudson said to Jack. "No way Trey would take drugs the night before a game. That game in Charleston was a big deal to him. I could barely even get him to take a drink at the party."

Jack took out his notebook, pen in hand. "Who do you think spiked Trey's drink?"

Hudson frowned. "I don't rightly know, but if you're asking me to guess, I'd say you should look at Jett. I was there when Trey died. I had a good seat right behind home plate and it seemed to me that while everyone else was scurrying around, trying to help Trey, Jett was standing off to the side, smiling."

"Smiling?"

"That's what I said. Now, I don't know for sure he was the one who killed Trey. There were others who benefited from his death as well, but if you're asking me to guess, that's who I'd say. If you do find out for sure who spiked Trey's drink, you be sure to let me know. Trey was my best friend, which means the son of a bitch who killed him and I have some business to attend to."

Jack thanked Hudson for his time and we left. I realized that if we did manage to identify the person who'd drugged Trey, we should probably give Deputy Savage a heads-up that Hudson might just cause them bodily harm.

"What did you think?" I asked Jack when we were in the car.

"I'm not sure. Hudson didn't say anything we didn't already know, except for the fact that Cranston had been known to have a temper and Jett seemed happy when Trey went down, but I could see he was choosing his words carefully. Almost as if he planned what he was going to say or, more importantly, not say. He knows something he's not saying."

"Seems like they all do."

Jack nodded. "Yeah. It does at that. At this point, based on what we know, I'd have to add Hudson to the not-a-suspect list, and Jett's a suspect."

"I thought we weren't going to add people to the suspect list until we spoke to them," I pointed out.

"I thought about that some more. I think we need to categorize everyone. We can move folks around later."

"Okay, so we have Coach Cranston and Jett on the suspect list and Heather and Hudson on the not-a-suspect one. Where should we place the others?"

"Hudson seemed to think Rena was okay with the fact that Trey was going to dump her, but I'm not so sure. I'd keep her on the suspect list for now and I'd add Candy, given what Clara said yesterday."

"So we have Coach Cranston, Rena, Candy, and Jett on the suspect list and Heather and Hudson on the not-a-suspect list so far."

"Yes. Until Alex speaks to Dexter, Parker, and Quinn, and we track down Portia, I say we leave them on the maybe list until we get a feel for where they stand or new information becomes available." Jack glanced at his phone. "We have over an hour before we meet with Candy. Should we grab a bite?"

"Maybe something light. I want to call Alex. I think he planned to meet with Parker and Quinn yesterday. I'm interested to find out how that went. Maybe he'll have enough information to move them off the maybe list and onto one of the others."

"Let's just grab coffee, then. We can have lunch after we talk to Candy."

Jack and I ordered our coffee to go, then settled on a bench lining one of the public beaches. I pulled out my phone and called Alex, who answered after the second ring.

"Hey, Jill," he greeted me. "I was just about to call you."

"Do you have news?"

"I spoke to both Parker and Quinn yesterday and wanted to fill you in on that, as well as get an update on anything you may have gathered."

"So far Jack and I have spoken to Coach Cranston, Heather Granger, and Hudson Dickerson. Based on those conversations, we've started assigning our suspects to one of three lists." I explained who we'd assigned to which list and why. Alex had several questions, most of which we didn't have answers for yet. Once we'd discussed the interviews Jack and I had conducted, we moved on to Alex's with Parker and Quinn.

"They were at the party as Rena Madison's guests," Alex said, confirming what Hudson had just told us. "Apparently, not only were Parker and Trey teammates but Quinn and Rena were good friends as well. According to Parker, he didn't get along all that well with Trey because he totally grabbed the spotlight, leaving Parker hidden in his shadow, even though he was a damn good ball player in his own right. He swears that although he wasn't a fan of Trey's, he'd accepted his lot and was focusing his sights on making a name for himself after he went pro. I didn't get the sense that Parker did anything to prevent Trey from playing in the charity game. Based on my impression of him as a person, I think we can move him to the not-a-suspect list."

"Okay. And Quinn?"

"Quinn is another thing entirely. Although Trey has been dead for over a year and Parker was drafted to a Major League team, it was clear she still held a grudge against him because she feels he robbed Parker of the college career he should have had. She didn't have anything nice to say about Trey; in fact, she spent quite a lot of time telling me what a lowlife loser he was, and how he not only stole Parker's thunder but the thunder of the entire team. She insisted he was only in it for himself and wasn't a team player. She was also angry that Trey was planning to dump Rena before he died. She wasn't shy about telling me Trey got what he deserved, but she swore she wasn't the one who drugged him."

"Do you believe her?"

"Actually, I do. She was very forthright in her anger. I didn't get the feeling at any point in our conversation that she was holding back or lying. While I think Quinn was angry enough to want to do harm to Trey, my gut tells me that she isn't the one who spiked the drink. If the drink was even spiked; we don't know for a fact that it was, and I'm not sure we'll ever be certain unless we find someone who knows exactly what occurred and is willing to admit it."

"I guess you're right. For now, let's just move Parker to the not-a-suspect list and leave Quinn as a maybe. Were you able to get in touch with either Rena or Dexter?" I asked.

"I spoke to Dexter on the phone. I'm heading north later in the morning and plan to meet with him this afternoon. I'm hoping to hear back from Rena as well. Either way, I should be back in time for the group meeting. By then, I hope we'll have enough information to narrow things down so we can focus on trying to prove what happened."

"What about Jett?" I asked. "He seems like a strong suspect, but I'm not sure how we're going to track him down if he isn't in Florida."

"I have some feelers out. We'll find him."

"Okay, great. See you when you get back."

I hung up and filled Jack in on the parts of the conversation he wasn't able to follow. "It looks like Quinn and Dexter are the only two left on the maybe list, but Alex should have a better feel for where he falls by the end of the day."

"What about Portia?" Jack asked.

"Oh, yeah. I forgot about her. Do we even know if she's still on the island?"

"I don't know, but maybe Candy will. Let's add her to the maybe list for now."

******

Unlike Hudson, who seemed happy to talk to us, Candy greeted us with a look of mistrust. She began the interview by reminding us that she only had a few minutes, and despite Jack's attempts to charm her, she wouldn't smile or even look us in the eye. Her answers were carefully considered, the information she was willing to share both sparse and guarded.

Jack started off by asking her about her friendship with Heather, then segued into questions regarding Hudson and her relationship as a couple with Trey and Heather. While she was a lot more closemouthed in her responses than Heather had been, the information she shared ran along similar lines.

"I understand Trey's girlfriend, Rena, was at the party the night before Trey died," Jack said.

The comment appeared to make Candy mad, which seemed to loosen her self-control quite a bit. "She shouldn't have been there. The party was for Trey's Gull Island friends, to celebrate his accomplishments. Trey wasn't thinking right when he invited his college friends. If you ask me, their being there ruined the whole thing."

"It seemed Heather handled the fact that Rena was with Trey better than could have been expected."

Candy shrugged. "Heather didn't want to seem petty. She put on a good face, but I know it hurt her that he brought another girl. He wasn't even planning to stay with her, so I don't know why he bothered to bring her to the island and introduce her to his friends. In fact, once he introduced her around, I don't think he spoke to her the whole night."

"Who did Trey hang out with?" Jack asked.

"Hudson and some of the other guys from the high school group. They were drinking and having a good ol' time, which, given the circumstances, didn't sit quite well with me."

"Circumstances?" I asked.

"Trey was going to leave Gull Island for good. He was going to ruin everything."

"Surely you knew he was headed for the Major League."

Candy shrugged. "Things happen. Plans don't always work out. Trey wouldn't have been happy living in some big city, far away from everyone who loved him. He might have been disappointed at first if the baseball thing didn't work out, but in the end, he would have been happier staying right here on the island."

I glanced at Jack, who was hiding a frown. He paused before asking the next question.

"We know Trey died due to the drug mixture that was in his system, combined with the extreme stress that may have been brought on by such an intense game. We've heard Trey might have been slipped the drugs rather than knowingly ingesting them."

"Yeah. I've heard that."

"Why do you think someone would slip drugs to Trey?"

Candy shrugged. "Can't say as I rightly know. Are we done now? I need to get back to work."

Jack nodded. "Yes, we're done for now, but we may have additional questions as our investigation continues. Would it be all right if we called you should we feel the need to speak again?"

"I really don't know anything and I'm a very busy person. Besides, it seems to me you ought to let Trey rest in peace. It was a terrible thing, what happened to him, and stirring things up again is only going to create a hardship for those who loved him."

"If Trey was murdered, don't you want to see his killer identified?" I asked.

"Don't see what good that would do. He's gone and there's nothing anyone one can do about it now. I really do need to git."

Jack offered her a smile. "Thank you for speaking to us."

Candy returned to work and Jack and I headed to his car. We decided to have lunch at Gertie's, so he headed in that direction when we left the grocery store where she worked.

"Candy seemed to have a rather unrealistic concept of how things were going to work out with Trey," Jack said as he pulled onto the main road.

"Yeah. She really did seem to have latched on to the perfect-life dream she'd hatched up with Heather. I wonder if she wasn't the one to slip Trey the drink so he'd get sick, miss the game, fail to be drafted, and stay on the island."

"Missing one game wouldn't have prevented Trey from being drafted," Jack pointed out.

"You and I realize that, but Candy seems to be somewhat delusional. Maybe she really thought she could create a situation where he would come back to the island and get back together with Heather, and everything would return to the way it was supposed to be."

"Yeah, maybe. We should definitely keep her on the suspect list."

"I know Alex wants to figure this whole thing out, but there were a lot of people at that party who seemed to have both motive and opportunity to put the drugs in Trey's drink, if that's what happened. I'm beginning to think we may not be able to do it without a confession or someone who saw what happened and will talk about it."

"This is a tough case," Jack agreed. "I guess all we can do is try to narrow things down a bit. If Trey's drink was drugged, at least one person knows about it. If we ask enough questions, that person may let something slip."

"Yeah, maybe. If nothing else, I feel as if our interviews are giving me a clearer understanding of who Trey was as a person. Gertie has lived here a long time and seems to know most folks. Let's ask her opinion of the people on our lists—at least the ones who lived on the island. I've found she has a pretty good feel for who people are at their core."

Chapter 7

Gertie's was packed with the lunch crowd when we got there, so Jack and I hadn't had a chance to pick Gertie's brain, but I did drop off a copy of the photo of the young couple, and I mentioned I might be back at some point to ask her a few questions. Once we left the café, Jack dropped me off at the resort so I could pick up Blackbeard and my car in anticipation of my visit with Garrett. I'd made a point of bringing the bird to see Garrett at least once a week since I'd been on the island because I knew how very much those visits meant to them.

"Man overboard, man overboard," Blackbeard said the minute he saw Garrett approaching us in his wheelchair.

I was glad Blackbeard had found his voice and to see the smile on Garrett's face too. I hoped spending some time with Garrett would bring Blackbeard out of his slump.

"How ya doin', big guy?" Garrett asked as I released my hold on the bird and allowed him to fly onto his shoulder.

"Not a hitter, not a hitter."

Garrett looked at me with a question on his face. "Have you been watching baseball movies with Blackbeard?"

"No. We've been investigating Trey Alderman's death, though, and Blackbeard has been listening in on our discussions."

"Investigating his death? Thought that case was closed."

"It is, but Alex is writing a book about Trey's baseball career and the circumstances surrounding his death."

"Man overboard, man overboard."

Garrett glanced at Blackbeard. "Yes, I'm afraid so. Trey collapsed just like I did when I had my stroke. I was lucky and pulled through, but poor Trey wasn't so lucky. It's a shame what happened. Kid was definitely too young to have a heart attack."

"The consensus is that there were drugs in Trey's system that, when combined with the stress of a close game, resulted in heart failure. So far, we have conflicting reports as to whether Trey took the drugs voluntarily or they were slipped in his drink without his knowledge. To be honest, I'm of the opinion that unless someone who knows what really went down and is willing to talk about it, it's possible we won't be able to solve this one. Still, we owe it to Alex to give it our best shot. I'm hoping we can wrap it up before the holiday. Which reminds me: I'm making Thanksgiving dinner and would love for you to join us if you feel up to it."

"I'd like that very much. I haven't been home since my stroke. I'm anxious to see what you've done with the place."

I smiled. "And I'm anxious to show you everything. I think the cabins came out really well. Six are finished and three more are underway and should be done after the first of the year. I've had a lot of interest from writers wanting to rent the cabins on a weekly basis. I'd prefer longer-term residents, but I suspect there aren't that many looking for a more permanent living arrangement, so I'm thinking of advertising short-term rentals in January."

"I know short-term rentals seem like a lot of work, but I think after you get into a routine, you'll find there are benefits. But it's totally up to you. I want you to consider the resort your own."

"Thanks. I appreciate that, but you still own the resort and I very much welcome your opinion. As for Thanksgiving, I'll have Jack pick you up on his way out to the resort. He has a truck he doesn't drive all that often, but it'll work perfectly to transport your wheelchair. Now that you're doing better, we should arrange for you to visit more often."

"No place like home, no place like home."

Garrett chuckled. "I spoke to my doctor about that when I was at the hospital having those tests. He thinks if I continue to progress the way I have, I may be able to consider physical therapy as an outpatient."

I was surprised but happy to hear it. "Are you thinking of moving back to the resort?"

Garrett hesitated. "The idea has crossed my mind, although I'll never be able to run it again. The doctor said I'll always need a certain amount of help, so living alone probably isn't in the cards. But living at the resort, where there are others to help me with meals and transportation, could very well be an option. Having said that, I don't want to be a burden to anyone."

"You wouldn't be a burden," I assured Garrett. "You're my brother. If you want to come home and the doctor agrees, I'll be more than happy to do whatever it takes to make it happen. The big bedroom on the first floor is empty, and there's a bathroom right next door. I'm not a contractor, but it seems that with a little modification we can create a door large enough to accommodate your wheelchair and give you direct access to the bathroom from the bedroom."

A look of longing crossed Garrett's face. "It would be good to be home again. Let me think about it a bit. Even if it does work out, it won't be right away. I'd want to be sure I had the strength to get myself in and out of my chair on my own. My upper body strength is returning, but it has a way to go."

"I'll be thrilled to have you whenever you're ready. George will be thrilled to have you back where you belong and I'm sure Blackbeard would love to have you at home again."

Blackbeard reached around and kissed Garrett on the cheek. I had a feeling the boys would both be very happy to have things back to normal.

"Now, you mentioned a photo you wanted me to look at?"

I handed it to Garrett. "I know you were little more than a child when the woman most likely stayed at the resort, but it occurred to me that she may have been a friend of the family and you may have seen her at other times."

Garrett stared at the photo. "No. Neither person in the photo looks familiar."

"I think the woman is called Francine, just because I found this photo with letters addressed to someone by that name."

"It's too bad Dad has taken a turn for the worse. He would have been the one to ask about her."

Our father had left Garrett and his mother when he was very young, and although he'd somehow found time to enter a relationship with my mother long enough for me to be born, he was never around when I was growing up either. I wished I'd had the chance to get to know him before his dementia got so bad he no longer remembered who anyone was.

"I'd hoped he'd work his way back to us," I said.

"It isn't looking good." Garrett reached out and took my hand. "The doctor doesn't think he has much time left. He could pass at any time and mentally, I'm afraid he's already gone."

I glanced down at the floor to quell sudden tears. I didn't know him, but he was still my father, and it made me sad that his time on earth was nearing an end. "During the brief period when his mind cleared, did he happen to share with you his end-of-life wishes?"

"Actually, he did. He made it clear he didn't want a fuss. He wants to be cremated and his ashes spread at sea. He doesn't have a lot to leave to anyone, but he did say he had a few dollars to take care of that."

"Did the doctor think there was any chance his mind would clear before the end?"

"He didn't say, but it seems unlikely. I don't suppose it's impossible. If that does happen, I'll be sure to call you right away."

******

After our visit, I headed back to the resort. When I arrived, I found Clara sitting on the sofa with Agatha in her lap, chatting with Victoria, who was thumbing through the photos Jack had left for Clara to look over.

"Kill the cat, kill the cat," Blackbeard squawked.

Agatha hissed at him, so I placed Blackbeard on his perch, near the back of the room.

Victoria chuckled. "I see Blackbeard has found his voice."

"He started talking the minute he saw Garrett," I replied. "I guess he just misses him."

"That's understandable."

"How's your brother doing?" Clara asked as I sat down.

"He seems to be doing better. I've invited him for Thanksgiving."

"I'm looking forward to meeting him." Clara beamed. "I've felt his presence in the house since I've been here. It will be nice to put a face with the vibe."

"Will all the writers be here for the holiday?" Victoria asked.

"I've had a chance to ask everyone except Brit, and so far, everyone's accepted the invitation. I'll talk to Brit when I next see her. Gertie's coming too, and possibly bringing a date, and George plans to invite Meg from the museum."

"Anyone else?" Victoria asked.

"I've invited Jack, of course, and Rick Savage said he'd get back to me."

"I'm having dinner with him tonight; I'll ask him," Victoria offered.

"I'm glad you decided to have dinner with him and I appreciate you speaking to him about Thanksgiving. If everyone I've invited comes, there'll be twelve of us. This will be the first Thanksgiving dinner I've hosted. I'm nervous, but I'm really looking forward to it."

"It should be a lot of fun." Victoria smiled.

"I see you've been looking at Jack's photos. Have you found anything interesting?" I asked.

"Maybe," Victoria answered. "For one thing, the photos taken at the party were extremely random."

"What do you mean?" I asked.

"They aren't typical party photos. No one is posing or looking at the camera. It's more as if the photographer had a purpose other than capturing memories with their friends. I called Jack to ask where he got them. He said most of the ones from the party were from a Facebook page owned by someone named C. Menow."

I frowned. "See me now?"

"That's the way I read it," Victoria answered. "The page has been dormant since the day Trey died, so I checked the email address associated with it. The account's no longer being used. I had Brit run a trace on the account to see if she could find the real name of the page owner. C. Menow is the only name listed. As far as Brit and I could tell, the name's a fake."

"How did Jack find the page in the first place?" I wondered.

"The person who posted the photos used plenty of tags, so when Jack entered Trey's name in his search engine, the page came up along with a bunch of others. There were so many that initially Jack just surfed around, stopping to print photos or articles that seemed relevant or interesting. It wasn't until after I had him go back to find the specific page he copied the photos from that he noticed the name on the account."

"Were there other posts on the Facebook page than the photos from the party?"

"There were, and all the photos related to Trey in some way. In addition to those at the party, there were photos of Trey playing baseball in high school and college."

"So C. Menow most likely went to all his games."

"Perhaps," Vikki said, "or got the photos from other sources and posted them on the page. It's hard to know for certain. There were also photos of Trey's friends, and some of him attending parties and social events in addition to the party the night before he died."

"Sounds like Trey had a stalker."

"That would be my take," Victoria agreed.

I looked at Clara. "Did anything stand out when you looked through the photos?"

"I feel quite certain C. Menow is the additional player I referred to on the first night we discussed the case," Clara answered. "That doesn't mean C. isn't one of the people already on the list and it doesn't mean C. is the person who drugged Trey. C. Menow is a troubled individual, and the existence of the Facebook page is a piece of the overall puzzle. I studied the photos associated with the Facebook page a bit more closely, though, and there are a couple that jumped out as being more significant than the others."

"Okay. Which ones?"

Clara picked up the pile of photos that had been sitting on the sofa between her and Vikki. She sorted through them, eventually picking out two and handing them to me. "What do you see?" she asked.

The first was a group shot of six people—four men and two women, smiling and laughing, none of whom I recognized—standing, chatting. Naturally, there had been other people at the party in addition to the suspects, but I wasn't sure why Clara had singled out this photo over all the others.

"Is there someone in the photo we should be paying attention to?"

"Yes, I believe so."

"Okay. Which one?"

"The one who only casts a reflection."

I looked at the photo again. It took me a minute, but eventually, I realized there was a mirror on the wall behind the group. Reflected in the mirror was the image of the person who'd captured the photo in the first place. The photographer held a large phone with a black case in front of their face, their identity further masked by a black hoodie pulled over their head. It was impossible to tell who the photographer was other than, based on the shoulders, they had a slight frame.

"Someone who was there must know who this is," I said as I continued to study the photo for any detail I might have missed.

"Wearing a black-hooded sweatshirt to a party doesn't seem an obvious choice," Vikki agreed.

"Do you think this is C. Menow?" I asked.

Clara shrugged. "I'm not sure. The photographer may have noticed their own reflection in the mirror when they took the photo, but it seems to me that whoever posted the photo to the Facebook page was deliberate in doing so, meaning *they* noticed it. If the poster was also the photographer, I have to assume they wanted to be identified."

"If they wanted to be identified, they should have taken off that hood so we could get a look at their face," Vikki said.

"If the person who took the photo is the one who posted it, my sense is they wanted to be seen despite being invisible," Clara responded.

"And if they continued to go unnoticed?" I asked.

"I suppose at some point they'd need to do something that would force the subject of their obsession to finally take notice."

"Something like putting drugs in his drink," I concluded.

"Perhaps."

I thought about the people we'd already spoken to. Heather had seemed to be open to speaking to us, willing to help where she could. Maybe I'd have Jack call her to ask if she knew who'd worn a black hoodie and taken photos at the party.

I set the photo aside to consider the second image Clara had handed me. This one was of Trey standing behind the bar that had been set up for the party. Hudson and a man I didn't know were sitting on barstools across from him, apparently chatting with each other, but Trey was looking at someone or something over their heads. It was impossible to know what he was looking at, but the expression on his face could only be described as haunted.

"I wonder what he's looking at," I said aloud.

"I don't know. Maybe nothing," Clara answered. "My sense is that although he's in a room filled with his friends, he feels alone."

"He seems to be smiling and having fun in the other photos," I pointed out.

"That's true," Clara agreed. "But my sense is that he's wearing a mask. I believe this photo shows his true face."

"Wow. For a party, it seems like there was a lot of deep stuff going on," Vikki observed.

"Yeah." I nodded. "There does seem to be a lot going on. The question is, how does any of this relate to Trey's death?"

No one answered, I imagine because no one had any idea.

"By the way," Vikki said after a long pause, "I called a friend of mine who works for the feds and asked him to look at your photo."

"You asked someone from the FBI to look at an innocent photo of a young couple most likely taken fifty years ago?"

"Like I said, he's a friend. The photo's pretty old and he can't do anything in an official capacity, but he's going to dig around a bit to see if anything pops. If the man in the photo is Paul, we know he was probably in the military. I'm sure there must be another photo of him somewhere. It's a long shot, a really long shot, but I figured it didn't hurt to ask."

"This guy must be a really good friend of yours if he's willing to go to all that trouble for a very long shot."

Vikki grinned but didn't reply. I didn't have to ask to know the FBI agent was another one of her conquests.

Chapter 8

I called Jack, who agreed to call Heather again to ask about someone wearing a black hoodie to the party. We also agreed on the time he'd pick me up for dinner that night, to a new restaurant on a neighboring island he'd been wanting to try. I'd been resisting the idea of dating Jack for weeks, but now that I'd finally taken the plunge, I realized I'd been crazy to fight it in the first place. Jack was kind and honest, as well as brave, handsome, and intelligent. He was everything I'd ever wanted in a man, which made me wonder what in the heck I'd been waiting for.

After I hung up I untied Blackbeard from his post and headed out the back door to enjoy a bit of fresh air. It was a perfect fall day, crisp and sunny with only a hint of a breeze in the air. I'd been so busy lately that I hadn't had much time to enjoy the fall color that had begun to fade but still lingered in some areas.

Blackbeard seemed content to ride quietly on my shoulder as I passed the small cabins dotted around the property, heading toward the white sand of the nearby beach. The turtles were gone, but I could still see the roped-off areas where they'd had their nests. When I'd first moved to the island and taken on the responsibility of both the resort and the wildlife that made its home there, I remembered feeling completely overwhelmed. But I'd taken my responsibilities seriously and learned what I needed to, and now I found I was looking forward to next spring, when the turtles would return to lay their eggs.

"What a beautiful day," I said aloud as the waves from the calm sea gently rolled onto the shore. I took a deep breath and allowed the serenity around me to chase the tension from my body. "It's so peaceful and quiet on the island now that the shorter winter months are near."

"No place like home, no place like home."

"You're right about that," I said to Blackbeard. "I really do hope Garrett is able to move back to the resort with us. I'm sure you'd enjoy having him around every day."

"Man overboard, man overboard."

"Yes, I know Garrett has been away since he's been sick, but it seems like he's doing better. I guess I should mention that Garrett is considering moving home to the others before Thanksgiving. I'm sure they'll all welcome him into our little family, but it would be best that they knew what we were thinking before he comes for dinner." I dug my bare feet into the sand as the warm water lapped over them. "I can't imagine how hard it's been for him to have to give up the life he loved so much."

"Grass is greener, grass is greener."

"Yes, sometimes people do move because they're chasing after something better, but in Garrett's case, I think the grass is greenest right here at the resort."

I paused as the photo of Trey flashed into my mind. In the beginning, I hadn't found him to be particularly sympathetic, but the photo Clara had shown me seemed to portray something more than the self-centered jerk I'd believed him to be. There was no way for me, or anyone, to know what he was thinking at that moment, but I'd experienced a moment in my own life recently that had allowed me to imagine what he might have been feeling. When the photo was taken, Trey was a couple of months away from the draft that would bring about a huge change in his life. I'd assumed, as had most of the people who'd known him, that being drafted would be a good thing that would allow him to realize his dreams, but it would also require him to leave his old life behind. I suppose the achievement of that dream might have seemed bittersweet.

"I guess we should head back," I said to Blackbeard. "I have a date tonight and I need to get cleaned up."

"Captain Jack, Captain Jack."

"Yes, with Captain Jack. He's pretty great. I can see why you're so fond of him."

"Secret kisses, secret kisses."

I smiled. The thought of stolen moments and secret kisses had been simmering at the back of my mind all day.

******

The restaurant, which was perched on a bluff overlooking the ocean, turned out to be a very nice steak house featuring fresh seafood and melt-in-your-mouth fillets. Jack ordered a nice bottle of wine while I looked over the menu, finally deciding on a small fillet and a petite lobster tail. Jack ordered steak and crab and we both started with a salad.

On the drive there, Jack had told me he'd spoken to Heather about the individual in the black hoodie. She didn't remember anyone at the party wearing a hoodie of any color, although, she said, she likely wouldn't have unless the person had stood out for some reason. He'd brought up C. Menow and Heather had sworn she had no idea who that was and had never seen the Facebook page, though she agreed to look at it when she got home that evening and would let Jack know if anything about it stood out to her.

I shared with Jack the conversation I'd had with Alex just thirty minutes before he'd picked me up. He'd had a long chat with Dexter and he seemed well over his adoration for Trey. Alex felt he hadn't said or done anything that would indicate he was responsible for his death. I thought about Dexter and his reputation for being a nerd in high school. In many ways, a man with above-average intelligence and below-average social skills was a good candidate for becoming obsessed with another person to the extent they might stalk and photograph them. I had no proof that Dexter was C. Menow, but I'd looked him up online and found he had a slight build. Of course, by the time of the party, Dexter was a senior in college and might have worked through his socially awkward phase, no longer having the need to follow Trey around. Still, I couldn't quite bring myself to take him off the maybe list. If it turned out Dexter was C. Menow, I'd be inclined to add him to the suspect list despite Alex's impression of him.

Jack and I had agreed that once we reached the restaurant we'd put shop talk on hold and attempt to have a discussion of the more personal kind.

"It looks like Garrett will be coming for Thanksgiving dinner," I said after a brief, awkward silence in which we'd both struggled for something to talk about.

"That's great. He must be doing better."

"He is. There's even a possibility he'll be able to move back to the resort permanently after the first of the year. Then he could continue his physical therapy as an outpatient."

"That's wonderful, but surely he hasn't recovered to the point where he can resume management of the resort."

"No. He most likely never will be able to run the place again. But he's getting around better with the wheelchair, and while he'll always need a certain amount of help, he seems to be on his way to living a somewhat independent life. I want to remodel the downstairs bedroom and bath so he'll have a suite that will accommodate his wheelchair."

"That's a great idea. You'll need a ramp at both the front and back door, as well as one from the deck to the yard. How about if I come by tomorrow to help you get started? We should have the front ramp and access to the downstairs bathroom in place by Thanksgiving."

I raised a brow. "I appreciate the offer, but Thanksgiving is in five days."

"It'll be tight, but I know a few guys who are looking for work, and I bet they'd be willing to take on a rush job. I was going to have them paint the newspaper building, but this is a bit more important. Leave it to me. I'll make sure everything is ready for Garrett when he comes home for the first time."

Words couldn't express how grateful I felt. I tried to find a way to tell him, but in the end, I leaned over and just kissed him on the cheek.

Our salads arrived and our conversation segued into different types of salad dressings and then the locations of the best meals we'd ever eaten. From there, we drifted to the letters I'd found.

"I gave them to Vikki, so I haven't had a chance to go back over them. I'm intrigued by the hidden box, but the likelihood of finding someone who might have stayed at the resort more than fifty years ago when all we have to go on are a photo and some letters seem like a pretty big long shot."

Jack swallowed, then set down his fork. "You might want to speak to Edna Turner. She ran the library before she retired twenty years ago and seems to be very knowledgeable about local history. I interviewed her recently for an article I wrote and found her to be deeply entrenched in the community. She seems to know everyone who's been around for any length of time and is in her midseventies at least, so she would have lived on the island when you suspect Francine was staying at the resort."

"Thanks for the lead. Maybe we can set up an interview after we get Alex's case wrapped up one way or another. I'm trying not to get distracted. Alex and Trey deserve our full attention."

"I agree. And the letters can certainly wait a few more weeks."

Our conversation drifted back to food for some reason, and by the time the main course arrived, we'd settled into a comfortable banter that was personal but not too much so.

"I know we said no shop talk during dinner, but isn't that Portia Sinclair with Brooke Johnson?" I whispered to Jack as we neared the end of our meal.

Jack and I had first met Brooke when we were investigating a recent death and its link to an eleven-year-old cold case that had turned out to be extremely complex, with a lot of things to consider once everything had been unraveled. Brooke was a wonderful person, a respected teacher, a loving mother who was pregnant with her third child, and a willing contributor in the community. She'd also been caught up in a situation from which the writers had been able to untangle her.

"I think it is. I left a message for Portia earlier, but I never heard back."

"I hate to interrupt their dinner, but I'd be interested in getting her take on things."

Jack hesitated. "Why don't we just introduce ourselves and see if we can arrange a meeting with her for tomorrow?"

We skipped dessert and paid the bill, then headed to Brooke's table on our way out.

"Jill, Jack, so nice to see you both," Brooke called out. "This is my friend, Portia Sinclair."

Portia had a frown on her face. "Are you the Jack who wanted to speak to me about Trey?"

"Guilty as charged." Jack smiled.

"Are you two working on another mystery?" Brooke asked, before turning to Portia. "Jack and Jill helped me out with something I was involved in not long ago. I'll vouch for the fact that you can trust them." Brooke looked back at me. "If I can help in any way, just holler. I owe you guys more than I can ever repay."

I thought about the photos taken at the party. Brooke was five or six years older than Trey and his friends, but she'd lived on the island her entire life, so she'd probably know the identities of at least some of the partygoers.

"We'd like very much to pick your brain," I said. "Tomorrow?"

"I have church activities early in the day, but I should be available by three-thirty. Why don't I meet you at the newspaper at four?" Brooke turned to Portia. "Will you come with me?"

Portia hesitated.

"It'll be fine. I promise," Brooke encouraged her.

Portia glanced at Jack, then nodded. "Okay. But I really don't know anything."

"That's okay," Jack assured her. "Jill and I are grateful for any help either of you can provide. We'll see you tomorrow at four."

We left the restaurant and Jack gave the valet runner our ticket. We stood hand in hand, looking out over the expanse of moonlit ocean while we waited for Jack's car to arrive.

"It's early yet," he said as he wrapped his arms around me from behind and pulled me into his chest. "Would you like to come back to my place for a nightcap before I take you home?"

I leaned my head back and rested it on Jack's body. I couldn't remember the last time I'd felt quite so content. It could have been the wine we'd had with dinner, but I suspected it was something more. I turned so I was facing him, put my arms around his neck, then leaned forward to kiss him softly on the lips.

"I take it that's a yes?" Jack asked.

"It's very much a yes."

Chapter 9

Sunday, November 19

When I came downstairs the next morning, George was sitting at the kitchen table with Clara with a pot of coffee and a basket of homemade muffins. They offered to share with me, so I pulled up a chair and poured myself a cup of the hot brew.

"George has news," Clara said as I took my first sip.

"What kind of news?" I asked.

"News about Trey Alderman. Tell her, George. Tell her your news."

"Tell her George, tell her George," Blackbeard parroted.

George glanced at the colorful bird with a look of amusement on his face. "Give me a chance. She's barely sat down."

"What's your news?" I asked.

"It's really quite juicy," Clara interrupted before George could say anything.

"I'm all ears," I persuaded. "What'd you find out?"

"I found an article in a low-budget gossip magazine that was published just four weeks before Trey's death. It seems a young woman named Melanie Carson, who went to the same college as Trey, claimed he was the father of her unborn child. Trey denied having ever slept with her, and the whole thing had seemed to go away, but a reporter claimed to have found evidence that Trey's father had paid Melanie to disappear, never to bother Trey or his family again."

"Do you think the reporter was making the whole thing up? I mean, you can't trust what you read in those rags."

"Initially, I didn't give the article much credence, but my curiosity got the better of me and I decided to see if I could track down Melanie Carson. I eventually found her living in Savannah, and when I explained who I was, what I was after, and why I was after it, she agreed to an interview. I made the trip yesterday."

"And...?"

"Melanie had her baby and seems to be doing just fine. She insists it's Trey's, that he was the only man with whom she'd engaged in sexual relations for more than six months before her pregnancy, so there's no doubt in her mind. When she told Trey she was pregnant, he didn't deny being the father, though he made it clear he wasn't looking to be tied down with a wife and child. He offered to help her out financially if she wanted to have an abortion. A couple of days after she spoke to him, Mr. Alderman showed up. He explained to Melanie that knocking up some random girl could hurt Trey's reputation at a very critical time in his career and offered her a lump sum of cash if she and the baby would simply disappear. At first, she turned him down, but the next thing she knew, Trey had publicly denied being her baby's father in front of a group of mutual friends; in the end, she decided to take the money. She left school to avoid a scandal and went to live with a good friend until after the baby was born. She claims she never talked to any reporters, that very few people even knew about the pregnancy, so she had no idea where the reporter got the information that was printed."

"Are we thinking this somehow played into Trey's death?" I asked.

"Initially, I didn't think this young woman's pregnancy had anything to do with Trey's death. She seemed content with her current situation and struck me as the sort to make the best of whatever situation she happened to find herself in. Then I found out the friend Melanie went to live with was Dexter Parkway."

"Dexter? How did Melanie and Dexter even know each other?"

"They met at a summer camp when they were in middle school. They were both smart and, at the time, socially awkward, so they became fast friends who kept in touch and helped each other get through the difficult high school years. It seems Dexter visited Melanie at the University of South Carolina. By this time, she'd grown into her own and was quite beautiful. While he was there, he ran into Trey, and he was the one who introduced them to each other. According to Melanie, she was immediately drawn to

Trey, and he seemed interested in her as well. After Dexter returned to his college, Trey and Melanie got together in a physical way. Trey was dating Rena, so Melanie agreed to keep their short affair a secret. When Melanie found out she was pregnant, she told Trey, and the rest you know."

I took a minute to let this all sink in. "So Dexter most likely not only resented Trey for the way he'd treated him all those years when they both lived on Gull Island, but I imagine he also felt responsible for what happened to his friend. He introduced them, after all. I can imagine a scenario where he was furious at the way she was being treated and decided to go to the party where he knew Trey would be and spiked his drink to render him unable to play in the game the following day."

"That's the gist of my theory as well." George nodded.

I paused before I continued. The theory had merit. Alex hadn't thought Dexter could be guilty, but he didn't have this piece of information. "I think you might be on to something. Let's present this to the group tomorrow night."

"Will Alex be back by then?" George asked.

"When I spoke to him yesterday, he said he planned to be. I'm pretty sure everyone will be here. Jack and I have an interview with Heather's friend, Portia, this afternoon. We don't consider her a suspect, but she was at the party, so she may have seen something. We're also working on an interesting theory dealing with someone who was using the alias C. Menow."

"The person with the Facebook page," Clara joined in.

"Yes. We're looking at a couple of different angles."

"I'm anxious to hear what you've found," George said. "It seems this mystery, like most, has multiple layers in need of careful peeling."

Clara turned and looked toward the front door. "Someone's here."

I hadn't heard anything, but maybe enhanced hearing was part of Clara's gift. "It's probably Jack and some of his friends. Garrett's coming home for Thanksgiving, so he's seeing to a ramp and an enlarged doorway for the downstairs bathroom."

"That's wonderful." George smiled. "I've been hoping the old chap would be able to get out a bit. He seemed to be getting antsy the last time I went to see him."

"He's pretty excited about the prospect. We're hoping that with a little help with everyday tasks, eventually he can move home permanently. But he has a way to go yet."

"I've been so excited since you first mentioned it and I can't wait to meet your brother," Clara added. "The house has already told me that he has a kind soul and a giving nature."

"The house is right. He's really great."

George added, "I spoke to Meg Collins and she's accepted my invitation to dinner."

I smiled. "Great. Vikki texted me to let me know Rick Savage is on board too, so only Gertie's date is tentative."

******

I went over to check in with Gertie while Jack got the guys he'd brought with him started on the ramp. He'd be tied up for an hour or so. Now that it looked like pretty much everyone was onboard for the holiday dinner, I was beginning to get nervous about having everything ready. When I entered the café, Gertie was standing behind the counter talking to Mayor Betty Sue Bell, who was just finishing her breakfast.

"Morning, Gertie, Betty Sue," I said as I walked toward them.

"Mornin', suga," Gertie responded.

"Heard you've been running around stirring things up again," Betty Sue teased with a smile on her face.

"You know me; I'm quite the rabble-rouser," I responded. "Although today I'm here to chat with Gertie about Thanksgiving."

"Gertie told me you're hosting dinner out at the resort."

"You're welcome to join us if you don't have plans," I said.

"I'm going over to my neighbors', but thanks for the invitation." Betty Sue returned her attention to Gertie. "I have a client in twenty minutes, so I best get going. Call me later and let me know what day you decide on for your cut and curl."

"Will do. Have a good day, now."

I sat down at the counter after Betty Sue got up.

"So, you want to talk about Thanksgiving?" Gertie asked.

"So far, it looks like everyone is coming, and Garrett's going to be able to come home for the holiday as well, so if you bring a date, that will bring us up to twelve."

"Garrett's gonna be there? Well Lordy be, I'm happy to hear that. He must be doin' better."

"He is. In fact, it may even work out for him to move back to the resort in a few months. Nothing is certain yet, but we're hoping. Jack's at the resort right now, having a ramp and a wider bathroom door installed in the house."

"You got yourself a good one there."

I grinned. "Yeah, I did. So, about Thanksgiving…Is there anything I need to do or buy before we get together tomorrow to do the big shopping?"

"I think we can get everything we need tomorrow, and then we'll make the pies on Wednesday. Might want to put together a centerpiece for the table. I noticed the general store has seasonal decorations you could use if you don't want to make anything."

"A centerpiece is a good idea. I'll stop by to get something on my way home."

"How's your investigation going?" Gertie asked as she wiped the counter. "I know you said you wanted to chat when you were here for lunch yesterday."

"I think it's going pretty well. It looks like Mortie was on to something with the whole intentional-drugging angle. The more people we speak to and the more information that comes our way, the more convinced I am that Trey's accidental death wasn't an accident at all."

"Mortie usually knows what he's talkin' about. Any suspects?"

"A few. I know you've lived here for a long time; you must know some of the people we're looking at. Do you mind if I pick your brain a minute?"

"Pick away, darlin'."

"What about Candy Baldwin, or I guess she's Candy Dickerson now?"

"Candy's a suspect?"

"Right now, she is."

"I guess I'm not surprised. Candy might have a sweet-sounding name, but if you get in her way, there's nothin' sweet about that girl. She's a pretty little thing and she seems devoted to Heather, who really is a sweetie, but Candy has definite ideas about things that don't always line up with the reality the rest of us live with. And if you challenge those ideas, she'll tear you a new one."

"So you think she could have spiked Trey's drink?"

"I don't know that she did, but yeah, given enough incentive, I think she could have. 'Course, she probably wasn't the only one with a grudge. Trey tended to let his success go to his head. Guess that happens. I know he had a fallin' out with his parents and wasn't hardly speakin' to them when he died. You want a cup of coffee?"

I glanced at the clock. "Sure. I have time."

Gertie poured me a hot cup, then set the cream in front of me.

"Do you know what the conflict Trey had with his parents was about?" I asked.

"Seemed to me it had to do with a girl. His mama didn't go into detail, but I did hear her say Trey's daddy was madder than a cat in hot water about trouble Trey had gotten himself in to. I guess he and his dad had words, and as far as I know, the issue between them never was resolved."

It probably wasn't my place to say anything about Melanie Carson, but if I had to guess, Trey and his father most likely had fought over the baby he'd fathered. "That's sad. It's so hard to lose a child under any circumstances."

"That it is, suga, that it is." Gertie paused, then added, "You know, you might want to have a chat with Reverend Thompson as long as you're lookin' into things."

"I don't think I've met him. Was he Trey's pastor?"

"When he was a young'un. His family worshiped at the Baptist Church for a lot of years, and it seems to me if there was somethin' goin' on with Trey, he might have been inclined to seek council. 'Course, he was a cocky sort once he got older, so I suppose it's entirely possible he figured he had everythin' under control."

I thought of the haunted look on Trey's face in that photo and realized speaking to the family pastor might not be a bad idea at all.

"How's your search for the woman with the letters goin'?" Gertie asked. "I've shown the photo to a few folks, but no one seems to know who either person might be."

"I haven't had a lot of time to work on it, but so far it seems like a dead end. Vikki has a friend in the FBI who's going to poke around a bit, but I'm not expecting much. I figure my best bet is to find someone locally who was around back then and might remember something. I know it was a long time ago, but there are quite a few folks on the island who are lifetime residents. Someone must remember something."

"You know, you might want to speak to Deke Manning. Deke's a lifer who's been on the island for more than seventy years. He's retired now, but he used to own a butcher shop. Now, offhand, I don't know why a butcher and a guest at the resort would be acquainted, but I don't suppose it would hurt to ask."

I grabbed a pen from my purse and wrote down his name on a napkin. "Jack suggested a woman named Edna Turner might be able to provide a lead."

"Yup, Edna would be a good one to talk to. Should have thought of her myself. And as long as you're making a list, you should add Roland Carver. He was the mayor years ago. Oh, and Clint Brown. He used to own a real estate office and he seemed to know a lot of folks."

"Anyone else?" I asked.

"Not off the top of my head, but I'll think on it some more, and I'll keep showin' the photo around."

"Thanks. Jack and I agreed to put Alex's mystery to bed before we spend much time looking for Francine and Paul, but the more I think about them, the more curious I become."

******

I called Jack when I left Gertie's to let him know I was going to stop by to speak to Reverend Thompson before I came back. I'd never met him and had no reason to believe he would share personal information regarding Trey or his family with me, but it couldn't hurt to chat with him just in case he had something he wanted to share.

The Baptist Church was in the center of town, near the library. It was a small building with a steeple and a bell tower that was built on a large lot that had been nicely landscaped with a lawn and a colorful flower garden. The Sunday service for the day was over at eleven and it was now close to noon, so I wasn't sure the pastor would even still be there, but Gertie had suggested I check the small office to the left of the main building, where Reverend Thompson was likely to be tending to church business.

"Reverend Thompson," I said to the older gentleman with gray hair and faded blue eyes after poking my head in through the open door.

"Yes. Can I help you?"

"My name is Jillian Hanford."

"Garrett's sister?"

I nodded. "I was hoping to speak to you for a few minutes about some research I'm doing for a friend of mine who's writing a book."

He smiled. "Please come in and have a seat. How's Garrett doing? I'm afraid I haven't taken the time to stop by to chat with him for more than a month."

"He seems to be doing a lot better these days. He's even planning to come home for Thanksgiving dinner."

"That's wonderful. I'm so happy to hear that. How can I help you?"

"One of the writers who lives at the resort, Alex Cole, is writing a book about Trey Alderman's life as it relates to his baseball career, including his death during the ball game in Charleston. I was just speaking with Gertie Newsome, who suggested I speak to you."

"I see. Was there something specific you wanted to know?"

I hesitated. "I'm not sure exactly. When I first began researching Trey's life, I found him to be a confident and somewhat arrogant young man. But I recently came across a photo of him, and in it the smiling, cocky young man appeared more distracted and detached. More than that, he looked haunted. I guess I wonder if there was something going on in his life that wasn't readily apparent."

"I'm afraid I hadn't spoken to Trey since he left the island to attend college, and even if I had and he had shared his concerns with me, I wouldn't be at liberty to discuss that information with anyone else. I will say, however, that Trey had a depth to him that those looking only at his actions might miss entirely. He liked to play the arrogant athlete who only needed to cock his finger for others to come running, but the reality is that Trey felt things a lot more deeply than others would imagine. I don't find it at all hard to believe that the course his life had taken, while quite fantastic, had left him feeling unbalanced and out of sorts."

"I understand Trey had a falling out with his parents before he died."

"That's my understanding as well. As I indicated before, though, I'm not at liberty to discuss such things."

I stood up. "I understand." I turned to leave. "The initial police report indicated Trey's heart attack was due to recreational drug use the night before he died. My writers' group has found reason to believe he didn't take the drugs voluntarily. In your opinion, did Trey seem the sort to take a bunch of drugs the night before a big game?"

"No. Trey was quite serious about his career—but keep in mind I hadn't spoken to him in several years, so I can't speak to his mental state at the time of his death."

"Thank you for your time."

"Tell Garrett hi for me. I'll try to get by to see him in the next few weeks. That brother of yours is a good man."

"Yeah. He is."

I headed back to the resort. I wasn't sure what Jack had planned between now and four o'clock, when we were supposed to meet with Portia and Brooke, but he probably had something in mind. I wanted to stop by the general store to look at decorations for the Thanksgiving table, and I should prepare a meal for the Mystery Mastermind meeting tomorrow night. Maybe I'd make tacos. It had been a while, and they were easy and would feed a crowd.

******

By the time I reached the resort, Jack and his friends had already begun to frame the ramp that would allow Garrett to enter the main house through the front door despite the four steps leading up to the front porch. Luckily, once you reached the porch, the front entry was already double wide and level with the decking.

"Wow! You've already made a lot of progress," I said to them.

"We should have this finished by the end of the day. The doorway into the downstairs bedroom and then from the bedroom to the adjoining bath will take a bit longer, but we should have it ready by the time Garrett arrives for Thanksgiving," Jack responded.

"I think it's going to mean a lot to him that everyone pitched in to make him feel at home."

"How did your talk with Gertie go?" Jack asked.

"She didn't have a whole lot of new information, but it's always nice to get another perspective. I was thinking about going to the general store, but I wanted to check with you first to see if you had plans for us between now and our meeting with Brooke and Portia."

Jack lifted a board and held it in place while one of the others nailed it into place.

"I don't have anything arranged other than to get the ramp done and make a supply list for the doorways. If you need to run to the store that's fine with me."

"Okay, great. I want to pick up something for dinner tomorrow night and maybe a centerpiece of the table. I shouldn't be too long."

"You might want to check with Victoria before you go. She was looking for you. I think she's out back."

"Okay, thanks. I'll see you in a bit."

I went around to the back of the house, where I found Victoria sitting on the deck overlooking the ocean. I pulled a lawn chair around and sat down beside her.

"Oh good; you're back. I wanted to tell you about my date."

Based on the huge smile on Vikki's face, it seemed it had gone well.

"Rick and I had a wonderful time. We dined in a nice restaurant, then took a drive down the coast a bit and found a place to park."

"And...?" I asked the obvious did-they-or-didn't-they question without words.

"And we didn't have sex. Instead, we talked for hours. You were so totally right. Slowing things down after the way things started was the right thing to do. Not that I'd like to leave sex on the back burner for too long because I'm still me, but it was nice to make an emotional connection with Rick, not just a physical one."

I leaned over and hugged my best friend. "I'm so happy things are working out. Rick's a good guy and I think the two of you will be good for each other."

"Me too." Vikki grinned. "And how did your date with Jack go?"

"A little different from yours," I hedged.

"You slept with him!"

"Shh." I looked around to make sure no one was listening to our conversation. "Yes, I slept with him, and yes, you were spot-on when you wondered what I was waiting for."

"How was it?"

Now it was my turn to grin. It would take time for me to get used to the changes in my relationship with Jack, but as I engaged in girl talk with Vikki, I realized I was happier than I'd been in a very long time.

Chapter 10

Jack and I arrived at the newspaper office an hour before we were due to meet with Brooke and Portia. He'd spent the whole day working on the ramp and never had gotten around to finishing the article he needed for the next edition. I'd managed to buy the supplies for the tacos but hadn't gotten around to looking for a centerpiece, so I ran over to the general store to look for something to use while he made some phone calls. It was a nice day and the store was close by, so I walked the two blocks rather than hassle with borrowing Jack's expensive sports car.

I was halfway between the newspaper and the store when I heard someone call my name. I stopped and looked around but didn't see anyone until a flash of yellow caught my eye. I watched as Heather Granger wove her way through traffic to cross the street.

"Oh good, you heard me," Heather said, breathing heavily from the effort of her sprint down the street. "I was going to call you, but then I saw you from the window of the paint store and decided to catch up with you instead. Who knew a little thing like you could walk so fast?"

I chuckled. "I guess I was moving along at a brisk pace. How can I help you?"

"Candy called me this morning in tears. She said you and Jack are trying to stir things up that shouldn't be stirred. I tried to tell her that you were just looking for some answers to what exactly led to Trey's death, but she was adamant that I speak to you and get you to put a stop to the whole thing."

"Do you have any idea why she's so against our investigating the case?"

Heather shook her head. "Not a dang clue. The whole thing is very odd."

I frowned but didn't say anything.

"Candy's my best friend," Heather continued. "I love her like a sister, but she tends to get things in her head that she won't let go of. Her attitude about this investigation made me think back to the things that happened the night before Trey died. There were some oddities at the party that I'd all but forgotten. I'm not one to place blame, and I'm having a hard time believing anyone would intentionally hurt Trey, but now that things are coming back to me, I find I'm beginning to wonder." Heather paused and took a deep breath, then blew it out slowly. "What I guess I'm trying to work up the courage to ask is whether you consider Candy to be a suspect in Trey's death?"

"She's on our list, along with several others," I answered honestly. "We don't have anything definitive enough yet to single out any one person, but we've found some things we believe warrant further investigation."

"See, the thing is that while Candy does tend to be somewhat stubborn at times, I can't believe she would hurt Trey. She might have had a low opinion of him, but she knew I loved him and she had to know I would be devastated by his death. I can't believe she would do anything to cause me so much pain."

"What if she didn't mean to kill him? What if she just intended to make him sick enough that he couldn't play in the game?"

"Why would she do that?"

I shrugged. "Maybe out of revenge for hurting you, or maybe she believed if he couldn't play in the game he would lose his shot at the draft and come back to Gull Island where he belonged. I know that doesn't really make sense…"

"No." Heather shook her head. "It does. Like I said, Candy gets these ideas she won't let go of." She glanced out into the distance and then back at me. "If you find any sort of proof that Candy's the one who spiked Trey's drink, will you tell me before you confront her? I think things will go easier if I'm there when you speak to her."

"Sure. I can do that. And thank you for trusting me enough to share this with me."

"You and Jack both seemed so nice when we spoke before, and I talked to Portia, who told me that Brooke Johnson vouched for both of you. I know you're just trying to find out what happened to Trey and I respect that." Heather turned and looked behind her. "I best get back to the paint store. I left a basket full of supplies the clerk is gonna want me to pay for."

With that, Heather turned and jogged back in the direction from which she'd come.

By the time I continued to the general store, bought some items to make a centerpiece for the Thanksgiving table, and made it back to the newspaper office, it was almost four. I stored my purchases in Jack's car and quickly filled him in on my conversation with Heather.

"From her tone of voice and body language, did you get the impression she thinks Candy might have drugged Trey despite what she said?"

"I think she's beginning to wonder. I imagine that now that we've put the idea in her head that Trey might have been intentionally drugged, she must be going over things in her mind, looking at the situation from different vantage points. I bet it's strange for her to look, even for a moment, at people she's been friends with for most of her life as potential killers. Personally, I hope when we get to the end of this investigation we find Trey really did just make a bad choice and his death was no one's fault."

"I'm beginning to feel the same way. It seems like even if someone did spike Trey's drink, their intention most likely wasn't to kill him. It will be sad if someone's life is ruined because of a stupid decision at a welcome-home party."

Brooke and Portia showed up a few minutes later. Jack got them settled around the long table he used to sort and stack newspapers before briefly filling them in on exactly what we were doing, why we were doing it, and what we hoped to gain from our investigation. Once he gave them a chance to ask any questions they had, he motioned for me to go ahead with the interview while he took notes.

I pulled out the photo I had of Portia, Rena, and Heather talking at the party while Candy looked on. I passed it across the table to Portia. "Do you remember this?" I asked.

"Yeah. I remember it."

"And can you remember what you were talking about?"

"Seems like Rena was talking about Trey and what a total ass he'd turned into now that he was getting ready to head to the draft. Heather was trying to make light of things by letting Rena know not to take it personally because he had a history of dumping his women when it was time to move on to a new phase in his life. I thought it was strange that she was being so nice to Trey's girl, but Heather is a nice person and she wasn't looking for any drama."

"And what was your part in the conversation?" I asked.

"I was mostly just listening. I guess I might have agreed with what was being said a time or two. You know how it is at parties; you wander around a bit and jump in on any conversations you happen to come across."

"Do you remember why Candy wasn't part of the conversation?"

"I don't know for certain, but I'd say Candy didn't want to be part of any conversation having to do with Trey. She wasn't a fan."

"I asked someone else to look at the photo and she said she thought Candy looked scared."

Portia's brows rose. "Scared? Why would Candy be scared?"

"You know," Brooke joined in, "now that you mention it, she does look a little scared. When I first looked at the photo, I was thinking she was angry, but now that I look closer I see what Jill means." Brooke glanced at me. "Did you ask Candy what she was feeling when this photo was taken?"

"Not yet, but we intend to." I returned my attention to Portia. "Do you remember who took the photo?"

"No. I don't specifically remember anyone taking photos at the party, but everyone has a camera on their phone, so I guess there were people snapping shots throughout the evening."

I took out the photo of the group talking, with the reflection of the photographer in the mirror. "Do you know who this is?" I pointed my finger at the person in the black hoodie.

Portia picked up the photo and looked at it closely. "No. I can't tell. It is strange, though, that I didn't remember Walter was even there. Guess he must have popped in and I missed him."

"Walter?" I asked.

"Walter Farmer." Portia pointed to a tall man with dark hair who was standing in the group of people I didn't recognize.

"Who exactly is Walter Farmer?"

"Local guy. Works on a fishing boat. He was a grade ahead of me and Trey in high school. Real good baseball player until Trey went in for the tag when Walter tried to steal home base and he blew out a knee."

I frowned. "I imagine that must have caused hard feelings between them."

"Oh, yeah. Everyone said it was Walter that was gonna make the pros before he got hurt. He's a good guy and I'm sure he knew that one of the risks of playing so aggressively is that you might get injured, but there are those who say Trey intentionally hit him in a way to cause the most damage."

"So maybe he wanted Walter out of the way?"

Portia shrugged. "Some say. I don't know what happened for sure. Coach Cranston must not have thought Trey did what he did on purpose or he would have kicked him off the team."

"Do you think Walter held a grudge against Trey?"

"Don't rightly know, but he came to Trey's party, so I'm thinking not."

Brooke picked up the photo and looked at it more closely. "I know Walter. He's a friend of my husband's. I can't say for certain whether Walter believed Trey intentionally tried to hurt him, but Walter's a nice guy who doesn't hang on to anger from the past. I wasn't at the party, but based on what I know of him, if Walter held any anger toward Trey for what happened, he would have dealt with it years ago and wouldn't have let it fester into something ugly."

Based on the look on the man's face, combined with the overall mood of the group he was chatting with, I found I had to agree with Brooke's assessment that Walter probably wasn't at the party to exact revenge for a wrong that had occurred years before.

Jack asked Portia a few more questions, but it seemed she didn't know much more than anyone else did.

"I want to thank you both for coming," Jack offered as he wrapped up the interview.

"I was glad to help," Brooke answered. "Before I go, I wanted to ask you both about the tree lot."

"The tree lot?" I asked.

"Every year the high school booster club runs a Christmas tree lot to raise money for the school's athletic programs. As usual, I've been asked to organize the volunteers. I know neither of you attended high school on the island, but I hoped you'd be able to cover a few shifts. We open the day after Thanksgiving and stay open until Christmas Eve or whenever the trees are gone, whichever comes first."

"I'd be happy to help out," Jack offered.

"Me too," I added.

"Great. Once I put together a schedule I'll call you both with some shift choices. I try to get enough volunteers so no one has more than one shift a week, but that doesn't always work out."

"I can fill in as much as needed," I said. "As long as you don't schedule me for the day after Thanksgiving. I'm hosting a dinner and I think I'll need at least a day to recuperate."

"Deal."

Chapter 11

Monday, November 20

I expected the local grocery store to be busy, but I didn't think it would be so packed I'd find myself wishing I'd worn riot gear. "This is nuts," I said to Gertie as we pushed our way through the throngs at the meat counter.

"It used to be that you were fine shoppin' for Thanksgiving right up until Wednesday; then folks got wise to the fact they needed to come in on Tuesday to avoid the last-minute rush, and then Tuesday began to be just as crowded as Wednesday. I really thought we'd be okay today. Guess folks are comin' out earlier this year."

"I guess it's a good thing I don't have a busy schedule today. I have a feeling we're going to be here for hours."

"It's all part of the experience, suga. I find it's best just to relax and enjoy the ride. Not a lot you can do about hurryin' things up anyway."

Gertie had a point. There weren't a lot of shopping options on the island, so heading to another retail outlet wasn't an option. The crowd around us wasn't going to thin no matter how much I complained, so I may as well relax and enjoy the experience.

I took a step back to allow a woman with an overflowing basket and a crying baby to pass. "Tell me about the gentleman friend you've invited to Thanksgiving," I encouraged.

"Name is Quentin Davenport. He recently moved to the island after retiring from his job as chief medical examiner for Los Angeles County. He told me he worked a lot of hours, so he never married or had a family. I met him when he came into the café for lunch a few weeks back. It was slow that day, so we got to talkin', and we hit it off. We haven't gone out on a date yet, but he's been back for a meal on several occasions, so we've gotten to know each other a bit. I figured he wouldn't know anyone on the island yet and might be alone for the holiday. He was right grateful for a place to go when I asked him."

Gertie and I moved up in the line a few spaces after a second butcher came to the window. "He sounds really great. Does he know about Mortie?"

"No. I figured I'd wait to see how things develop before introducin' them. For one thing, Quentin seems kind of conservative. For another, Mortie gets jealous, and I don't need any trouble right off the bat. Last man I brought back to my place ran screamin' from the house after Mortie introduced himself in a less-than-friendly manner. Never did see him again."

"I imagine it must be challenging to live with a jealous ghost."

"You aren't wrong about that. There are times when Mortie gets on my last nerve. Even considered movin' a time or two, but I guess in the long run I'd miss the guy."

"He sounds like a real character. I'd like to meet him someday."

"Mortie doesn't always come out when folks are around, but you can stop by sometime. You never know who he'll take a likin' to."

I nodded toward the counter. "It looks like we're next."

Gertie ordered a fresh turkey she'd have delivered to the resort on Wednesday. Once that was accomplished, we headed to the center of the store to pick up the canned and boxed goods. The produce aisle looked like Grand Central Station at rush hour, so Gertie and I decided to tackle that last.

"Do you think we should buy a couple of cans of whipped cream for the pies?" I asked.

"Cans? The only cream goin' on my pies is freshly whipped cream. We'll pick it up last. Grab a couple cans of black olives. Maybe three. And maybe some of those pickles as well. I thought we'd get some fresh veggies to add to the relish tray too."

"Do you want me to grab a couple of cans of gravy while I'm at it?"

Gertie rolled her eyes before explaining that any meal she cooked didn't include gravy one bought in a can. It seemed, I was beginning to realize, that there was a lot more to making a Thanksgiving dinner than I'd ever imagined. I was feeling just a bit overwhelmed as Gertie suggested we make the rolls on Wednesday, along with the pies. When she mentioned her plan to serve two types of potatoes and three different vegetable sides, I wondered if maybe we shouldn't invite additional guests to eat all this food.

"You okay with sausage stuffin'?" Gertie asked.

"Sure. I guess. Are there different kinds of stuffing?"

"There are as many different kinds as there are cooks makin' it. I mix it up from time to time, but I thought I might make my sausage stuffin' this year, unless you had somethin' else in mind."

"Sausage stuffing sounds good. Are you sure we need this much food, though?"

"'Course we do. Won't be enough for leftovers if we don't make a lot to begin with, and everyone knows that leftovers are the best part."

Given the fact that the only Thanksgiving meals I'd ever consumed had been eaten at a restaurant or a friend's house, I was fairly certain I'd never had Thanksgiving leftovers before. I found I was quite looking forward to them.

After we finally made it through the produce aisle and the mile-long line at the checkstand, Gertie and I took the ingredients that would be cooked at the resort on Thursday there before dropping off the items we would need to make the pies and rolls at the café. What I had expected would be a quick trip to the market had turned into a three-hour marathon and I was exhausted. It would have been nice to head home and take a nap before the Mystery Mastermind meeting, but I still needed to stop in to have a chat with Deputy Savage before the gang gathered that evening. He had texted earlier and asked me to come in when I had a chance.

******

"Do you have news?" I asked the minute I walked into his office.

"Actually, I do. As per your request, I asked for a copy of the original police report from Charleston PD and it finally came through this morning. Most of what's contained in the report parrots what we already know, but there was one item I found interesting."

"Okay, shoot," I encouraged.

"While reading through the original investigator's notes, I found a reference to a local doctor. There wasn't any information relating to the doctor other than a statement that the man investigating the case had followed up with him and found his conclusion to be unsubstantiated."

"When you say *local doctor*, do you mean he was a Gull Island local or a Charleston local?"

"Gull Island. He retired six months ago and moved away, but I know him well enough to have his new phone number, so I called and asked him about his involvement in the original investigation. He told me that at the time of Trey's death, he requested a copy of the toxicology report and was granted access. According to this doctor, who would like to have his name left out of things, he found evidence that supported the idea that Trey not only ingested drugs the night before, but on game day he ingested a large amount of caffeine, ephedra, taurine, and other ingredients you might find in an energy mix. It's his opinion, it was the energy mix that led to his death, not the drugs he took the night before."

"So why is this the first we're hearing about it?"

"The doctor communicated his opinion to the investigator at the time of Trey's death, who thanked him politely for the input but said the medical examiner's information didn't support the conclusion that Trey died from side effects relating to caffeine or any type of energy mix."

I tried to get my head around what Savage was telling me. "Why would the investigator want to cover up evidence?"

"I don't know that he was covering up evidence. It could just be that he didn't agree with the local doctor's opinion. Just because this particular doctor made the assertion doesn't necessarily mean he was right."

"Is the toxicology report part of the police report you have in your possession?" I asked.

"No. It wasn't included in what was sent over to me."

I let that sink in. It made sense that Trey's death would have been caused by drugs he'd recently consumed, but I didn't know a thing about drugs or drug interactions. I supposed it was just as likely drugs that had been sitting around in his system for a while could have killed him.

"So the question is, if the local doctor was correct and Trey ingested stimulants on the day of the game, did he take them willingly or was he slipped them without his knowledge?"

Savage sat back in his chair. "Unless we end up getting a confession from someone, I'm not sure how we can ever know. There are a whole lot of unanswered questions surrounding Trey's death. Did he willingly engage in drug activity at the party or was he slipped drugs without his knowledge? Either way, was the local doctor correct in his assertion that Trey ingested additional stimulants on game day or was the investigator correct in believing the doctor was mistaken? If Trey ingested additional stimulants on game day, did he take them of his own volition or was he slipped the energy mixture? If he took them of his own volition, did he know he already had drugs in his system from the previous evening? If he was slipped the energy mixture on game day, did the same person slip him the drugs at the party, or were there two different people involved? And if there were two people involved, did they each know what the other had done? Lastly, did they know the combination of drugs was likely to be lethal under the right set of circumstances?"

"That's a lot of *if*s."

Deputy Savage leaned forward and placed his elbows on the desk in front of him. "I'm not sure we'll ever be able to sort this out."

"It does sound like we need to get someone to talk. The writers are meeting tonight. Alex spoke to everyone who doesn't currently live on Gull Island and George has been looking in to some things as well. I'm hoping if we put our heads together, we can come up with some answers, or at least narrow things down. You know you're welcome to come to the meeting if you'd like."

"I appreciate that, but I think it would be best given the uncertain situation with the temporary sheriff that I not participate in meetings designed for civilians to try their hand at solving crimes. I have plans with Victoria later, so if there's anything I should know, she can relay the information."

I grinned. "I understand things between you two are going well."

"Did she tell you that?"

"Yes, she did. And she seems very happy. I know Vikki can come off like a barracuda at times, but she really is sensitive and has a huge heart. I guess what I'm trying to say is that I'm glad you're working things out, but if you hurt her, you'll have me to deal with."

"Duly noted. And just so you know, I really care about Victoria. The last thing I want to do is hurt her."

"Good." I stood up. "I should get going; I'm making dinner. If you come up with any ideas on what to do next, I have some time to talk tomorrow. I'm pretty busy on both Wednesday and Thursday, though."

"Understandable. Do you want me to bring something on Thanksgiving?"

"Just yourself. I'm looking forward to a relaxing day with the people I love the most."

Chapter 12

It was nice to have the whole family together sharing a meal. The tacos were a hit, it seemed, and the atmosphere in the room was of happy anticipation. Jack was chatting with Alex and George, so I decided to join Vikki, Brit, and Clara, who were huddled together at the end of the long dining table.

"What are we talking about?" I asked as I sat down next to Vikki.

"Your mystery of the photo in the wall," Vikki answered. "Clara and I were filling Brit in."

"The whole thing is just so romantic," Brit said with a wistful tone in her voice. "It seemed so obvious from the letters that Paul was deeply in love with Francine. I bet he spent every minute of every day dreaming about their life together after he was discharged."

"She may have been a married woman," I pointed out.

"That's what we were discussing when you came over," Vikki said. "There was definitely someone in the picture named Tom, and it seemed obvious Paul was worried about the fact that this Tom was being discharged, but if you read the letters from oldest to most recent, you'll find that Tom isn't mentioned at all until the last few letters."

"I guess you're right. I read the letter on the top first, which was the most recent one. Paul spoke about Tom quite a bit, so I guess in my mind he was in the picture the entire time. You think he wasn't?"

"It's hard to say," Vikki answered. "I've gone through the letters many times, and if you read them in order you experience a beautiful love story between a man named Paul and a woman named Francine who loved each other very much but were torn apart by the war and Paul's duty to serve his country."

"The whole time I was reading the letters I kept wishing we had Francine's responses to Paul," Brit joined in. "It seemed she must have loved him based on Paul's comments to her, but in truth, we only have half the story. We don't know for certain if she shared his feelings."

"She kept the letters and hid them in the wall," Vikki said. "I have to believe if she didn't share his passion, she wouldn't have done that."

"I held the locket earlier," Clara said. "I could feel the love, the longing, the sorrow, but I also felt fear. I'm not sure Francine was afraid of this Tom who's mentioned in the later letters, but she was afraid of something."

"As I said before, the first letter I read was the most recent one sent," I said. "In that letter, Paul mentions that Tom is about to be discharged and will be coming home. Paul is fearful of how Tom will take the news of their relationship and worries that

Francine will be on her own with Tom until he's discharged in six months. I read that to indicate that Tom was Francine's husband, or perhaps her fiancé. It's hard to know for certain, but I get the feeling she was committed to him in some way, that her dalliance with Paul took place outside the structure of that relationship. Did anyone have a different impression?"

"The first mention of Tom is three letters before the end," Vikki told me. "Until that point, Paul and Francine were the only two people in the picture. Then, in the third to the last letter, Paul writes that he's worried because he found out Tom had been discharged and was being sent home. He doesn't go into a lot of detail. Then, in the next letter—the second to the last that was sent—he tells Francine that the situation with Tom has been on his mind a lot and reminds her that it's imperative that Tom not find out about them. Then, in the last letter, Tom is almost ready to return home, and you can sense Paul's growing concern. Now, on one hand, it seems like Tom night be Francine's husband. But Brit thinks maybe Tom is someone who has power over Francine and would have an opinion as to who she fell in love with but wasn't a love interest. Someone like a father or a brother."

I paused to consider that. "Why did you think that?" I asked Brit.

"Because while Paul expresses fear that Tom is coming home and Francine will have to deal with him on her own, he doesn't express jealousy. I just think that if he was in love with Francine and her husband or fiancé was about to reenter her life, he might be feeling at least a twinge of jealousy that Tom would be spending time with her, possibly making love with her, and he wouldn't."

"I guess that's a good point," I admitted. "I'm committed to focusing on Alex's case, but when it's over, I really do want to see if I can track down Francine to get the rest of the story."

"Fifty years is a long time. It'll be hard to find someone who might remember some random woman from that long ago," Brit warned me.

"True. But we know she stayed at the resort. We don't know for how long, but she hid possessions that must have had great sentimental value to her in the wall, so she must have stayed in the cabin longer than just a weekend."

"Probably," Brit agreed. "But even that's an unknown. Maybe she knew Tom was coming home and didn't want the things she'd hidden in her house, and also couldn't bring herself to destroy them, so she rented a cabin for the weekend and hid them there. There are a lot of variables to consider."

The group fell into silence. I could see that all the women in the room had been pulled into the mystery. It seemed likely we'd never have the rest of the story, but I assumed it was possible I could find a local old enough to remember someone who remembered Francine, or Vikki's FBI friend would find the man in the photo, who I assumed was Paul, in a military database. In the meantime, we had the death of a local baseball player to solve. It looked like everyone was finished with their meal, so I decided it was time to get on with the brainstorming session.

******

"Before we begin the sharing of information, I have some general announcements," I said. "First, Brooke Johnson is organizing volunteers for the annual Christmas tree lot that benefits high school sports. I told her I'd pass along the information and ask you all if you'd be willing to help. I have Brooke's number if you want to call her."

There was a general murmur in the room and it seemed as if everyone was at least considering getting involved.

"Second, while I'm pretty sure you already know Garrett will be joining us on Thanksgiving, I also wanted to mention that he's considering moving back to the resort at some point in the future. I'm sure you all noticed the ramp in front of the house and the work Jack is doing on the first-floor bedroom and bathroom doorways, but just in case you haven't gotten the whole story, the rest of the first floor of the main house at least will be made accessible as well. Garrett's returning home won't affect what we're building here in the least. He's very much on board with the idea of the writers' colony. Those of you who haven't met him yet will find he'll fit right in."

"I for one am thrilled he may be able to move home," George piped up.

"No place like home, no place like home," Blackbeard joined in.

"That's right." I glanced at the colorful bird. "There really is no place like home." I returned my attention to the group. "And finally, I wanted to let you know we'll have a new resident on December 1. We talked about her briefly at our last meeting; her name is Nicole Carrington and she's a true crime writer. I've since finalized things with her. I think it's likely she won't be interested in becoming a member of this group, but I'm sure we can welcome her with open arms; perhaps eventually she'll want to become part of our family."

"I'm anxious to meet her," Brit said. "Did she talk to you about the project she's working on?"

"No. Nicole seems to be a very private person. She told me she wasn't moving here to socialize but to do research for her project. I'm not sure how long she'll be staying and I think her plan is to keep her work to herself."

I paused a moment to see if anyone else had questions before I moved on. "Before we focus in on the case, does anyone have anything they'd like to share that isn't related to it?"

"I have something," Brit said. "I know I'm here to work on becoming a writer, which is going slowly, but I also decided to try my hand at acting, so I joined the community theater group."

We all congratulated her.

"Anyway," Brit continued, "my first production with that group will be the annual production of *A Christmas Carol* on December 21, 22, and 23, and I'd like you all to come. I have tickets, so you can buy them directly from me."

"I'll take one for sure," I said.

The others agreed.

"Anyone else?"

No one responded.

"Okay, then, back to Trey Alderman. Jack and I have worked out three lists in which we've grouped those we spoke to by the likelihood they spiked Trey's drink: suspect, not a suspect, and maybe a suspect. Our up-to-date lists are on the whiteboard.

Keep in mind, the lists are based strictly on the impressions Jack and I have gathered. I'm sure some of the names will be moved to other categories during the course of this meeting; this is just a starting point. I also want to add that I had a conversation with Detective Savage, who informed me that Trey may have consumed a large quantity of caffeine and other energy enhancers the day of the game."

"He isn't sure?" Alex asked.

"No. There are conflicting reports. A local doctor got hold of the toxicology screen, and he was the one who felt Trey consumed energy enhancers on the day of the game that may have contributed to his death. The investigator in charge of the case didn't agree with his assessment. It doesn't look like the matter was ever conclusively resolved, but I think we should keep that possibility in mind as we discuss things now."

I pointed to the lists on the board. "This is what we came up with. Let's see if we can narrow it down."

Suspect:
Candy Dickerson
Coach Cranston
Rena Madison
Jett Strong

Not a Suspect:
Heather Granger
Hudson Dickerson
Parker Wilson
Portia Sinclair

Maybe a Suspect:
Dexter Parkway
Quinn Wilson

I turned the floor over to Alex, who began to fill us in on the outcome of the interviews he'd conducted on his trip.

"I met with Parker and Quinn Wilson on my first day in New York," he began. "Both seemed to be forthright in their answers to my questions. If you remember, Parker was on Trey's team in college, and although he was a very good player himself, he didn't get the local or national attention he would have had Trey not stolen the limelight. Both Parker and Quinn attended the party thrown in Trey's honor as guests of Trey's girlfriend, Rena Madison. Rena and Quinn were best friends at that time, despite the fact that Quinn hated Trey."

"It seems odd to me that Parker and Quinn would have attended a party thrown by Trey's friends in his honor, even if Rena did invite them," Brit said. "I mean, it isn't like they knew anyone else who was going to be there. The game was in Charleston, and most of the players were staying there. Charleston is a great town with an abundance of nightlife. Why travel to Gull Island to attend a party for a man neither cared for?"

"I agree with Brit," Vikki said. "It doesn't make sense they'd go even if Rena invited them. What possible motivation could they have had?"

I thought about the photo of Quinn flirting with Jett while Parker looked on. "Unless they somehow knew Jett was going to be there and attended to meet him," I suggested.

"Why was Jett there?" Jack asked. "That makes even less sense than Parker and Quinn being there."

I looked at Alex. "Did you ever track Jett down?"

"He's in California, but I did speak with him on the phone. He told me he went to the party to meet Coach Cranston. It seems the coach and Jett's dad had spoken to each other and the coach was supposed to give Jett something he was to pass on to his father, but when Jett got to the party, Coach Cranston said he'd changed his mind. According to Jett, he left shortly after that; he didn't know anyone and wanted to turn in early to be rested for the game the next day. I asked him if he knew of a plot to drug Trey and he said he didn't, though he admitted that when Trey first went down, his reaction was joy intermingled with relief. He said he'd been chasing Trey his entire career and had built up quite a resentment against him."

"Did he say what it was the coach was supposed to give him for his dad?" I asked.

"He claimed he didn't know. His father and Coach Cranston seemed to have hatched up some sort of plan, but Jett said that ever since he was a little boy, his father had been extremely aggressive about making sure he came out on top. He knew he'd crossed the line in the past, but he felt helpless to do anything about it, so he'd learned to turn a blind eye and not ask questions he didn't want the answers to."

The room fell silent.

"Okay, what do we know?" Jack began at last. "We know Coach Cranston spoke to Jett's father at the game in Charleston thanks to the photo from the parking lot. We also have a photo of them standing side by side after Trey went down. Given the fact that

Mr. Strong didn't arrive in Charleston until the night before the game and we have no reason to believe he visited Gull Island at any point, we have to assume he isn't the one who put drugs in Trey's drink. He isn't on any of our lists, and I don't see a need to add him. If Jett went to the party to pick up something Coach Cranston had for his father, it sounds like the coach might have had something up his sleeve, but it most likely wasn't drugging Trey."

"Maybe he had an agreement with Mr. Strong that would have allowed him to get back at Trey for dumping him as his agent. But by the time Jett showed up at the party, he'd changed his mind about the original plan, deciding to drug him instead," George suggested.

"Good point," I jumped in. "And it sounds like Coach Cranston lied about knowing or having spoken to Mr. Strong. He said he didn't recall when Jack and I spoke to him, but I'm still not buying it."

"Okay, wait," Brit interrupted. "We started off talking about Parker and Quinn." She looked at Alex. "Did either mention what Quinn was talking to Jett about?"

"I hadn't seen the photo of Quinn talking to Jett when I first interviewed them, so I didn't ask about it. I asked Jett what he was talking to Quinn about and he said she wanted him to get her into a party he'd been invited to back in Charleston but they weren't. He told her he wasn't going, that he just wanted to go back to his hotel to get some sleep."

"What does your gut tell you?" I asked Alex.

"That while Jett, Parker, and Quinn all had reasons to want to see Trey fail, none of them drugged him. I haven't personally spoken to Coach

Cranston, but it does sound like he might have been cooking something up with Jett's dad. It also sounds like he changed his mind. At this point, I don't have a strong feeling that any of them are the person we're looking for."

"What if there were two people who gave Trey drugs?" Brit asked. "I realize we aren't completely sure Trey took energy enhancers on game day, but what if he did *and* someone slipped them to him without his knowledge the night before? Would that someone have to be Parker or Jett by the process of elimination? I doubt the others would have had access to Trey on game day."

We all took a minute to consider the possibility.

"Brit has a point," Jack eventually said. "Because we don't know if Trey was slipped energy enhancers on game day, maybe we should focus on what we *do* know: that Trey consumed drugs on the night before the game, most likely at the party. We haven't conclusively ruled out the idea that he took the drugs voluntarily, although most of the people Jill and I have spoken to have said he would never have done such a thing the night before a big game."

"Okay," I said, marker in hand. "Should we move both Jett and Quinn to the not-a-suspect list?"

There was some discussion before we decided that, for the purposes of this discussion, we should.

"That leaves Rena, Candy, and Coach Cranston on the suspect list. What about Dexter?"

Alex paused before he answered. "I spoke to him, and while he certainly didn't say anything to incriminate himself, I did pick up an odd vibe. He's brilliant, but he's still socially awkward."

"Still?" I asked.

"Yes. He has friends and he seems to be doing very well in his field of choice, but there was something about the way he wouldn't quite look me in the eye when he spoke to me. We met in his apartment and I noticed a photo on the shelf of Trey tossing a baseball. I asked him about it and he said Trey had been his friend and he kept the photo as a reminder of the person who'd once been an important part of his life. He seemed sincere, but then George told me about Melanie Carson. I remembered seeing a photo of a woman with a baby on the shelf too. I'd asked Dexter about it and he said it was of his best friend and his goddaughter. Now, I'm no relationship guru, but it seems to me that if Melanie and Dexter really are that close, Dexter would be furious at Trey after what he did to her. It doesn't fit that he'd have a photo of him on his shelf to this day."

"And Dexter would have had the knowledge to mix a drug cocktail that would make Trey sick the next day," Vikki reminded us.

"He does fit the profile of a person who would adopt the persona of C. Menow," Clara mused.

"I think we need to move him from the maybe list to the suspect list," I said.

The others agreed.

I stood back and looked at the whiteboard. "We have no one left on the maybe list. Heather, Hudson, Parker, Portia, and Jett and Quinn are all now on the not-a-suspect list. Does anyone see a reason to move any of them to the suspect list?"

Everyone agreed that, for now, the individuals were fine where they were.

"We have Candy, Coach Cranston, Dexter, and Rena still on the suspect list. Does anyone have cause to move them?" I added.

"While Coach Cranston and Rena certainly had motive to want to hurt Trey, my money is on Candy or Dexter," Clara stated. "There's something off about them. I think we should take a second look at both of them."

I looked at Clara. "When you saw the photo of Candy watching Rena, Heather, and Portia, you said she was scared. It's occurred to me that she knew Trey was going to be drugged and who was going to do it."

"That would be my guess as well," Clara confirmed.

"Dexter is up at Harvard, but Candy is right here on the island. I suggest we follow up with her to see if we can get her to tell us what she knows," Alex said.

"And someone really should try to figure out whether Dexter is C. Menow. If he isn't, who is? Jack added.

"I'll do that," Brit volunteered. "I've mapped the social media accounts of all the suspects already, so focusing in on one person will be easy. I'll look for any similarities between the C. Menow account and the accounts under Dexter Parkway's real name. If they're the same person, I'll find a way to prove it."

"Okay, great. I'll talk to Candy again," I said. "She wasn't very open to speaking to us the first time, but maybe she can be persuaded."

"I'll come with you," Clara offered. "I may be able to help."

"And I'll contact Melanie Carson again," George offered. "Maybe she knows something she didn't mention the first time we spoke."

"I'll have a chat with Coach Cranston," Alex said. "Maybe I can find out what he was up to with Mr. Strong."

"I'll go with Alex," Vikki volunteered. "I do have a way of getting men to talk. And I'll ask Rick if he knows anything more than he already told Jill about the doctor's report."

"Okay, great. Let me know right away if Deputy Savage gives you a clear answer one way or the other about the possibility of drugs being taken on game day. That piece of information could be a game changer." I glanced at the board, then back at the group. "It looks like we all have something to do. Should we meet again between now and Thursday?"

"It would be nice to get this wrapped up," Clara said.

"I agree. Let's plan to meet back here tomorrow night. Even if we don't have all the answers, we may be able to get a tighter focus."

I hoped Jack would stay for a while after the meeting was over, but he told me he'd been spending so much time working on Alex's case that he needed to put in a couple of hours this evening if he wanted to get the newspaper out on time. Vikki left to go over to Rick's, and Alex, George, and Brit all returned to their cabins, leaving me alone with Clara, who seemed to be having a conversation with Blackbeard.

"No, dear, I don't think that's quite right," Clara was saying to the bird.

"Sick sister, sick sister," Blackbeard seemed to be insisting.

"What are the two of you arguing about?" I laughed.

"This silly bird is trying to convince me that we need to find out about a sick sister," Clara answered. "I've tried to tell him there aren't any sisters involved in the mystery, but he's quite adamant."

"Blackbeard uses words and phrases he knows to communicate his thoughts. 'Sick sister' doesn't seem like a logical clue, but it might behoove us to keep it in mind."

"Very well. Agatha and I are going up to our room. We'll see you in the morning."

"Good night, Clara." I turned and looked at Blackbeard. "Are you ready to be tucked in as well?"

Chapter 13

Tuesday, November 21

The next morning, Vikki called me to say she had news. She wanted me to meet her in town for coffee. I asked her why she didn't just walk over to the main house and we'd have coffee here, but she said she wasn't at home. It seemed Vikki's plan to take things slowly with Rick had been abandoned in favor of speeding things up, but Vikki sounded happy, so I decided not to worry about her having spent the entire night with him. We met at Marina Coffee, a coffee bar that served the designer coffees Vikki preferred. After ordering our beverages as well as a couple of muffins, we took a seat in the back, where we wouldn't be overheard.

"What's up?" I asked.

"I heard back from my friend at the FBI."

"And…?" I leaned forward in anticipation.

"He wasn't able to track down Paul through military records, but he found Francine through police records."

I frowned. "Police records? She had a record?"

"Not exactly." Vikki placed her hand over mine. I could see the tears in her eyes. "Francine died. More accurately, she was murdered."

I took a deep breath and swallowed hard. "Murdered?"

"It turns out that Francine Kettleman, also known as Frannie K., was the fourth victim of the Silk Stocking Strangler."

I could hear my heart pounding as I tried to wrap my head around this.

"The Silk Stocking Strangler murdered thirteen women over a ten-month period in 1964 and 1965," Vikki continued. "All the victims were strangled with a pair of women's nylon stockings, and all thirteen bodies were found in cemeteries along the East Coast from Florida to Massachusetts."

"Oh my God. How awful. That poor women. Do you know exactly when Frannie was murdered?"

"On August 12, 1964."

"Just shortly after the letters stopped. Do you know where she was found?"

"A cemetery about fifty miles from here. My friend tracked down the original FBI report. Frannie, who was just twenty-one at the time, was living at the resort when she was killed. Garrett's mother, Lillabeth Hanford, was interviewed at the time, and she reported that Frannie had been living at the resort for a little over a year. Mrs. Hanford confirmed that Frannie was married to a man named Tom Kettleman, who happened to be the son of one of Mrs. Hanford's best friends, Vivian Kettleman. Vivian had recently passed away after a long battle with cancer. Shortly after his mother passed, Tom was drafted. He didn't have any family in the area, so Tom asked Mrs. Hanford to watch out for Frannie while he was away. He was supposed to be gone for two years, but he was injured and shipped back to the States after serving only fifteen months. He returned home just five days before Frannie was found dead."

"Wow. I had a lot of thoughts regarding how this whole thing would end, but I wasn't expecting this. It seems surreal."

"Yeah. I felt the same way when I heard. I almost feel as if I knew Frannie after reading Paul's letters to her. When my friend told me what had happened to her, I actually cried."

I took a sip of my coffee, allowing myself a moment to get my emotions under control. I'd never met the woman, hadn't even heard of her until a few days before, but I couldn't help but feel as if someone had punched me in the gut. To not only die so young but at the hands of a serial killer was beyond imagining.

"It's odd," Vikki said. "When you first showed me the letters and I realized Francine would be in her seventies by now, I half-expected she might have died along the way. Not that it's all that odd to live into your seventies, but I would think the odds are just as good you wouldn't make it that far. I wasn't expecting to be upset if we found out she was gone. I was more interested in learning how she lived. But this…To die young and in such a violent way. It makes me feel ill."

"I know what you mean." I took another sip of my coffee. "I still wonder what happened to Paul. He must have been devastated."

"Yeah. The poor guy really seemed to be in love. I don't suppose we'll ever know how his life turned out."

"Although now that we know who Francine was, and that she was a friend of Lilly Hanford's, maybe that will jog Garrett's memory and he'll remember something. I think I'll ask him about it at Thanksgiving. It couldn't hurt."

"That's a good idea." Vikki glanced at her phone. "I have to run. I'm supposed to meet Alex to talk to Coach Cranston, and then I have to fly up to New York to meet my agent about the production schedule for the first movie they're making on my book series. I'll be gone overnight, but I should be home by dinner tomorrow."

"Okay. I'll see you tomorrow. And thanks for going the extra mile to find out about Francine."

"No problem. I was curious too."

******

Clara was understandably upset when I told her what had happened to Francine. She asked if she could hang on to the locket in the hope of making a connection with Franny's spirit. I wasn't attached to the locket in any way, so I told her she could keep it as long as she wanted.

I'd called Candy and requested another meeting, this time with Clara and me. She wasn't thrilled with the idea, but she didn't refuse either. After a bit of negotiation, she agreed to let us take her to lunch on her break. There was an hour before we needed to leave the resort, and I was on my way out the door for a short walk when I ran into Brit.

"Oh good. I caught you," Brit said.

"What's up?"

"I think I found the proof we need to demonstrate that Dexter and C. Menow are the same person. I have my computer all set up in my cabin. Will you come over and look?"

"Absolutely. I've had a feeling this whole time that Dexter and C. Menow were the same person, although I'm a bit surprised he was still so insecure by his senior year of college. I understand he's quite brilliant."

"Yeah, well, sometimes an elevated IQ can act as a barrier to social normalcy."

I followed Brit into her cabin. She'd done a lot to make it her own; brightly colored paintings hung on the walls, a red coffeemaker sat on the counter, and red and white mugs hung from hooks under one of the cabinets.

"I love the sofa," I said as I sat down on the dark blue suede unit.

"Thanks," Brit responded as she sat down at her computer desk. "It was kind of a splurge, but I really, really wanted it. I'll probably be paying for it for the next five years, but it was worth it."

"It goes perfectly with your grandmother's quilt," I said, referring to the quilt, made from dark blue, bright red, and white squares.

"The quilt is the main reason I went with the red, white, and blue theme. A house just wouldn't be a home without Nana's quilt." Brit typed some commands into her computer. "Okay, this is what I found. I started off by looking through Dexter Parkway's current social media accounts. At first, nothing jumped out as odd, but then I noticed that he used #feelinit several times in his posts over the past few months. I went back and looked at C. Menow's posts to see if I could find a similar hashtag and found three instances where C. Menow used #feelinit. Now, that doesn't prove conclusively that the two are the same person, but it was a start. Once I had that piece of information, I looked at the dates the posts to C. Menow were added during the time Dexter would have been doing his undergrad work at Boston College. I found that with one exception, all the posts between the time Dexter would have gone off to college and Trey died were made either on the weekend or during the summer or school holidays."

"Yeah, but C. Menow could have posted from anywhere."

"True, but almost all the posts consist of photos with hashtags. The photos are all of Trey, so C. Menow would have had to have taken the photos when he was home from college."

"Maybe, but Trey was in college during that time as well. It could be that C. Menow lives on Gull Island and was only able to take the photos when Trey was home on break."

"That's a legitimate point. I did, however, find this one photo of Trey at the University of South Carolina." Brit scrolled through and pulled up a photo of Trey standing in front of the university library, speaking to a young woman who looked as if she might be another student.

"I wonder if that's Melanie Carson. George told me that Dexter went to visit Melanie, who also attended USC, and ran into Trey. He was the one who introduced them."

Brit hit Print and the photo spilled out. "I guess we should ask him. If this is Melanie, it would seem to me that Dexter has to be C. Menow."

Brit and I returned to the main house. George was on his way out but before he left he confirmed that the woman in the photo was Melanie Carson. Proving Dexter was C. Menow didn't also prove he was the one who'd drugged Trey, but it made him a lot stronger suspect. I called Alex to let him know what we'd found, and he agreed to call Dexter to confront him with the evidence we'd uncovered. While I had him on the line, he told me Victoria had worked her magic, managing to get Coach Cranston to admit that Jett's father had wanted him to give him a report he had that revealed Trey had tested positive for steroids in high school. Trey was a minor at the time, so the report, which had been made when the high school tested all its athletes, wasn't a public record. Trey had been suspended for two games, but no further action was taken. As far as the coach knew, Trey stopped using the steroids after his drug use was discovered.

Coach Cranston had indeed been hurt that Trey had dumped him, which was why he'd agreed to provide Mr. Strong with a copy of the report. It probably wouldn't have made a whole lot of difference by then, but Cranston knew image was important, and if it had gotten out that Trey used steroids while in high school, it could have created suspicion on possible current drug use. By the time Jett showed up to get the report, which the coach had insisted be picked up in person, he had changed his mind. He told Jett the deal was off, Jett left the party, and he assumed that was the end of it until Mr. Strong tracked him down at the game and they'd had words in the parking lot.

"So why were they standing next to each other when Trey went down?" I asked Alex.

"Cranston said he was watching the game and Mr. Strong came over to stand next to him just as Trey was coming up to bat."

"Did they speak?"

"Cranston said Mr. Strong apologized for being out of line, and the next thing he knew, Trey was down. He claims he was in shock after that and didn't remember much of what happened from then on."

I turned to Brit and Clara. "So now we know why Coach Cranston lied about having spoken to Jett's dad," I said. "I'm sure he didn't want to admit he'd even considered giving Mr. Strong the damaging report. We're fairly certain Dexter is C. Menow. I guess we just need to figure out who drugged Trey."

"It has to be Dexter," Brit insisted. "He was at the party and he had motive, not only because of the way Trey had treated him but how he treated Melanie and his own baby. Assuming he's C. Menow, we also know Dexter was obsessed with Trey in a way that goes way beyond normal hero worship. He also has the knowledge base to mix the drug cocktail given to Trey at the party. It has to be him."

I glanced at Clara, who had a thoughtful expression on her face.

"I don't know," she finally said. "My instinct tells me Candy is somehow involved. She either spiked the drink herself or knows who did it. I think once we're able to unlock the secret she has been hanging on to, we'll have our answers."

"Okay. Let's go meet with her." I glanced at Brit. "I'll fill you in when we get back. It would be really nice to wrap this up today; I'm going to be elbows deep in pies tomorrow."

******

Candy had wanted to meet in a little burger place near the store where she worked. By the time Clara and I arrived, she was already seated in one of the red vinyl booths. "Coffee?" I asked.

"No. I'm eight weeks pregnant and Doc says I shouldn't drink coffee. I'll just have a burger and water, if that's okay."

"Sure, and congratulations. I hadn't realized you were expecting."

"Not everyone knows yet. Just a few people, like Hudson's and my family. I didn't want to say anything until I was sure, but I guess it won't be long before I start to show."

"Yes, I guess it won't."

We ordered at the counter and Clara and I took the bench seat across from Candy. "Thank you for coming," I began.

"I told you before, I don't know nothin'."

"I know. But I felt maybe there was something you wanted to say before but didn't have the chance."

"It's all right, dear," Clara joined in. "I know you're frightened. I understand that fear. You want to tell us what you know, but you also want to protect someone. Someone who means a lot to you. Someone you'd never in a million years want to hurt."

Candy didn't respond.

"Is it Dexter you're protecting?" I finally asked.

A single tear slid down Candy's cheek. "It wasn't supposed to happen that way. It was a mistake. We would never have hurt Trey."

"We?" I asked.

"Me and Dexter. Dex was just trying to help. He didn't do nothin' wrong."

"Maybe you should start at the beginning," I suggested.

Candy used a napkin to dry her eyes. She took several deep breaths, then began. "Trey wasn't supposed to drink the spiked punch. Rena was."

"Rena?" I asked.

"She was ruinin' everything. Trey and Heather were meant to be together. Everyone knew that. When Trey broke up with her, Heather was so mad and so hurt. Trey shouldn't ought to have treated her the way he did. I was so mad at him for ruinin' everythin' that I could hardly stand it, but then he came home over Christmas durin' his junior year. Heather and me and Hudson were all at this party, and Trey walked in. I could see by the look in his eyes that he'd been missin' Heather, and I knew she was missin' him too. I was sure they were goin' to get back together and things would go back to the way they should be, but then Trey went back to school after New Year's and met Rena. When she showed up with him at the party that night, I was so mad. She shouldn't ought to have been there. Even Heather was bein' nice to her. It wasn't right."

I waited for Candy to finish. I was sure the only way I'd get my answers was to let her work through things at her own pace.

"I was so mad at Rena that night, I guess I wasn't thinkin' straight. I knew a guy who was there who sometimes had drugs to sell, so I asked him if he had any that would make a person really sick. He said he had somethin' that was fun to take and might lead you to do crazy, embarrassin' things. I thought that sounded good. He warned me it would lead to a nasty sort of hangover, but that seemed like a bonus. I bought some of the drugs and put them in a cup of punch and gave it to Rena, but she said she didn't care for it and gave it to Trey."

"And you were too scared to warn him not to drink the punch," Clara said encouragingly.

"I was so scared. I didn't know what to do. I knew I'd made a mistake and I wasn't sure if I'd get arrested or what. I figured the drugs couldn't be all that bad if people took them at parties, and even if Trey got sick, he'd be fine by the next day, but he wasn't. When I found out he wasn't goin' to play in the game because he was so sick, I told Dex what I'd done. He said he had somethin' he sometimes used when he had to study long hours, and it would help Trey feel better. He went to see Trey and offered him the energy mix. Trey really wanted to play, so he took what Dexter was offerin'. Dexter told him to only take one little pill, but after Trey died, Dex said he must have taken more than one."

"Why didn't you tell anyone what had happened?" I asked.

"Why? What difference would it make? Trey was dead and there was nothin' anyone could do to bring him back. I was scared that Dex and I might be in real bad trouble even though neither of us meant to hurt Trey. I asked Dex about it, and he said we should just keep it to ourselves. He had a degree to finish and I had a wedding to plan. Hudson and I got married that summer. Anyway, after a bit everythin' settled down until you all came around and stirred things up."

Oh, Lord. What a mess. The last thing I wanted to do was get Candy or Dexter into hot water. Dexter was working on his doctorate and had a promising career ahead of him, and Candy was newly married and pregnant. But I knew I really couldn't keep this to myself, so I did the only thing I could do: I called Deputy Savage and hoped for the best.

Chapter 14

Thursday, November 23

"I'd like to make a toast," I said as I stood at the head of the table at the first Thanksgiving dinner I had ever hosted. "When I came to Gull Island, my life was kind of a mess. To be honest, I only agreed to come as a means of escape and wasn't sure how long I'd stay. But after arriving in this magical place, I found that I not only had a brother who I consider to be a friend but an entire community of friends who feel like so much more. I love you all and I thank you from the bottom of my heart for helping me to find the family I've always prayed for."

"Hear, hear" everyone said.

"I also want to give special thanks to Gertie, without whom we would have been eating takeout. When I first came up with the idea to do this, I had no idea what I was getting myself in to."

"Thanks, Gertie," everyone called.

"I'd like to say something as well," Garrett added from his wheelchair. "After I had my stroke and the doctors explained my prognosis, I thought I'd never have the opportunity to set foot in this place again. But then Jillian came and gave me a reason to try to get better, and here I am, spending Thanksgiving in the place I love. I can't tell you how much it meant to me when Jack drove into the driveway in front of the house and I saw the ramp. Thank you all from the bottom of my heart."

"And you think you might move back in now that the doors in the downstairs bed and bath have been modified?" George asked.

"I'd really like to. I need to work out a few things with my doctors, but I think it might be a real possibility."

"No place like home, no place like home," Blackbeard parroted.

"You got that right, buddy," Garrett responded. "I've missed our conversations."

"Clara has been filling in in your absence," I assured Garrett. Suddenly it hit me. "Oh my gosh. Sick sister. Blackbeard must have been talking about Candy wanting to make Rena sick." I looked at the bird. "How could you possibly know?"

"Blackbeard knows a lot more than anyone realizes," Clara informed us. "Don't you, sweetie?"

"Shouldn't tell, shouldn't tell."

"What shouldn't you tell?" I laughed.

"Secret wishes, secret wishes."

"I guess we all have those."

The conversation paused as everyone passed overflowing dishes around the table and began to eat. I couldn't help but notice the way Rick's shoulder touched Vikki's, and the way Gertie was smiling at every word Quentin said. Clara was exchanging shy glances with Garrett, and I could feel Jack's heat next to my own body. There was no doubt about it; Cupid was in attendance at my first-ever Thanksgiving.

After a long day of baking pies and rolls on Wednesday and an equally long morning of preparing the meal, everything had turned out perfectly. Rick was in the process of working out a deal that would allow Candy to take responsibility for her part in Trey's death while continuing with her life. Dexter hadn't really done anything wrong other than cover up the fact that he knew Candy had inadvertently slipped Trey the drug that made him sick. He'd offered the energy mix to Trey, but there was nothing illegal in it, and Trey had taken it voluntarily. Dexter had warned Trey to take just one and Trey had made the choice to take more than he'd recommended.

It had been a tough week. Finding out that Francine had been murdered had affected me more than I'd expected. I'd talked to Jack about it, and he'd agreed to help me look in to the fifty-year-old case after Thanksgiving. The likelihood that the man who'd killed those young women was even still alive wasn't all that great, but the Silk Stocking Strangler hadn't been caught, and I wanted to bring Frannie's killer to justice if I could. Jack had warned me that it was going to be all but impossible, but I'd mentioned it to Vikki and Clara, who felt as I did, and we were going to bring the mystery to the entire group when we met next week.

"Looks like we did okay," Gertie, who was sitting to my right, whispered.

I looked around the table. Everyone was eating and chatting. "Yeah, it looks like we did at that. When you told me how much food you planned to make, I figured we'd be eating leftovers for months, but now that I see how much everyone is eating, I'm not sure we'll have enough for even one meal."

"We'll have enough. I kept some back, just to be sure."

"I think that might have been a good idea; almost everyone is on seconds and even thirds." I put my hand on my stomach and sat back. "I couldn't eat another bite."

"Don't forget about the pies."

Oh yeah, the pies. They did look good. Gertie had made pumpkin, pecan, chocolate, and apple, something for everyone.

"I guess I could make room for a small piece of pumpkin pie when everyone is ready. It's Thanksgiving, after all."

After everyone had finished eating, Jack, Alex, and George cleared the table while Vikki and Brit put away the leftovers. Quentin chatted with Rick and Garrett while Gertie made the fresh whipped cream and Clara and I sliced the pies.

"Are these the plates you want to use?" Meg asked as she took a pile out of the cupboard.

"Yes. Those are perfect. There are coffee cups in the next cupboard over. We may as well set them out as well."

"I really appreciate you inviting me," Meg said as she opened the drawers, looking for forks. "I usually go to my daughter's, but she went to her in-laws this year. When George asked me to come, I was so very grateful to have a place to go."

"You're welcome any time."

"You've put together a real nice family here."

I smiled.

Contentment settled in as I closed my eyes and listened for a moment to the chatter around me. I'd never had family holidays growing up, but I'd always dreamed of them. I'd longed for the sound of people talking and laughing as they worked side by side to put together a meal that would be enjoyed by all. I hadn't been entirely sure what to expect when I'd decided to host Thanksgiving dinner, but for the first time in my life, I knew exactly how magical a holiday meal with those you cared for the most could be.

http://amzn.to/2eLFowu

During the course of the remodel on one of the cabins at the writers retreat, the contractor finds a box hidden in a wall. Jill opens the box to find love letters writing to a woman named Francine more than fifty years ago. Jill decides to track down the woman to return the letters only to find that she was the fourth victim of the Silk Stalking Stranger, a serial killer who killed thirteen women in the mid 1960's. The strangler was never caught so Jill and the gang decide to dig into the mystery only to find that the fourth victim of the Silk Stalking Strangler may not have been killed by the Strangler after all.

Books by Kathi Daley

Come for the murder, stay for the romance.

Zoe Donovan Cozy Mystery:

Halloween Hijinks
The Trouble With Turkeys
Christmas Crazy
Cupid's Curse
Big Bunny Bump-off
Beach Blanket Barbie
Maui Madness
Derby Divas
Haunted Hamlet
Turkeys, Tuxes, and Tabbies
Christmas Cozy
Alaskan Alliance
Matrimony Meltdown
Soul Surrender
Heavenly Honeymoon
Hopscotch Homicide
Ghostly Graveyard
Santa Sleuth
Shamrock Shenanigans
Kitten Kaboodle
Costume Catastrophe
Candy Cane Caper
Holiday Hangover
Easter Escapade
Camp Carter
Trick or Treason – *September 2017*
Reindeer Roundup – *December 2017*

Zimmerman Academy The New Normal

Ashton Falls Cozy Cookbook

Tj Jensen Paradise Lake Mysteries by Henery Press

Pumpkins in Paradise
Snowmen in Paradise
Bikinis in Paradise
Christmas in Paradise
Puppies in Paradise
Halloween in Paradise
Treasure in Paradise
Fireworks in Paradise – *October 2017*

Whales and Tails Cozy Mystery:

Romeow and Juliet
The Mad Catter
Grimm's Furry Tail
Much Ado About Felines
Legend of Tabby Hollow
Cat of Christmas Past
A Tale of Two Tabbies
The Great Catsby
Count Catula
The Cat of Christmas Present
A Winter's Tail
The Taming of the Tabby
Frankencat – *August 2017*
The Cat of Christmas Future – *November 2017*

Seacliff High Mystery:

The Secret
The Curse
The Relic
The Conspiracy
The Grudge
The Shadow
The Haunting – *September 2017*

Sand and Sea Hawaiian Mystery:

Murder at Dolphin Bay
Murder at Sunrise Beach
Murder at the Witching Hour
Murder at Christmas
Murder at Turtle Cove
Murder at Water's Edge
Murder at Midnight – *October 2017*

Road to Christmas Romance:

Road to Christmas Past

Writers' Retreat Southern Seashore Mystery:

First Case
Second Look
Third Strike
Fourth Victim – *October 2017*

Rescue Alaska Paranormal Mystery

Finding Justice – *November 2017*

USA Today bestselling author, Kathi Daley, lives in beautiful Lake Tahoe with her husband Ken. When she isn't writing, she likes spend time hiking the miles of desolate trails surrounding her home. She has authored more than seventy five books in eight series including: Zoe Donovan Cozy Mysteries, Whales and Tails Island Mysteries, Sand and Sea Hawaiian Mysteries, Tj Jensen Paradise Lake Series, Writer's Retreat Southern Seashore Mysteries, Rescue Alaska Paranormal Mysteries, and Seacliff High Teen Mysteries. Find out more about her books at **www.kathidaley.com**

Giveaway:

I do a giveaway for books, swag, and gift cards every week in my newsletter, *The Daley Weekly* **http://eepurl.com/NRPDf**

Other links to check out:
Kathi Daley Blog – publishes each Friday
http://kathidaleyblog.com
Webpage – **www.kathidaley.com**
Facebook at Kathi Daley Books –
www.facebook.com/kathidaleybooks
Kathi Daley Teen – **www.facebook.com/kathidaleyteen**
Kathi Daley Books Group Page –
https://www.facebook.com/groups/569578823146850/
E-mail – **kathidaley@kathidaley.com**
Goodreads –
https://www.goodreads.com/author/show/7278377.Kathi_Daley
Twitter at Kathi Daley@kathidaley –
https://twitter.com/kathidaley
Amazon Author Page –
https://www.amazon.com/author/kathidaley
BookBub – **https://www.bookbub.com/authors/kathi-daley**
Pinterest – **http://www.pinterest.com/kathidaley/**

AUG 2 3 2017

South Lake Tahoe

Made in the USA
Columbia, SC
31 July 2017